Promises Are Made to Be Broken

Booker shook his head stubbornly. "Dewey, this is a small town, and it is my humble job to keep the peace. I will not allow the muscle of the rich people hereabouts to cloud my judgment on a case. And I refuse to be cowed by obscure threats and rumors about my own involvement," he added grandly. "Now. Suppose you do a little favor for me?"

"What's that, Bookie?"

"I'd like you to keep your own counsel on this whole affair."

"But, Bookie—"

"Sorry, Dewey. That's how it is." He smiled at her. "You know that I have the greatest respect for you."

"I know no such thing, Bookie. In fact, if pressed, I'd say that you think I'm a little bit off my rocker."

"Not at all. You are earnest and inquisitive. But this is a very serious police matter . . . Dewey. I want your promise."

"Bookie, honestly. I promise I won't bother you with idle speculation. There. Will that do?" She smiled brightly at him and departed.

The Dewey James Mystery Series From Berkley

A SLAY AT THE RACES
MURDER MOST FOWL
HOME SWEET HOMICIDE

A Dewey James Mystery

Home Sweet Homicide

Kate Morgan

BERKLEY BOOKS, NEW YORK

HOME SWEET HOMICIDE

A Berkley Book / published by arrangement with
the author

PRINTING HISTORY
Berkley edition / September 1991

ISBN: 0-425-12895-4

A BERKLEY BOOK ® TM 757,375
Berkley Books are published by The Berkley Publishing Group,
200 Madison Avenue, New York, New York 10016.
The name "BERKLEY" and the "B" logo
are trademarks belonging to Berkley Publishing Corporation.

PRINTED IN THE UNITED STATES OF AMERICA

10 9 8 7 6 5 4 3 2 1

For Beezer, Mouse, and Crocky Doodle,
whose liability is joint and several

1

"OUT-BACK-RIGHT, in-forward-left; that's right, count as you go, very good," said a sugary voice in the ear of Dewey James. "Now let's try a turnout: slow, slow, quick-quick. Very nice, Mrs. James. Just try to keep the *teensiest* bit more *tone* in the shoulder and upper arm. *That's* right." He let go of her hand momentarily, grasping her elbow with a sweaty palm. "*Now* we're getting it."

Dewey James recoiled inwardly at the clammy touch of the funereal Norman Fox, but she smiled politely and concealed her disdain. Why on earth had she ever agreed to take part in this farce? "Yes, I see. Er—thank you, Mr. Fox," she said.

"You stick with me," he pursued, beaming at her. "A few more evenings in my care and you'll be ready to paint the town. You'll be able to go anywhere—no more sitting alone in a corner, ashamed that you can't dance."

Even at sixty-odd years of age Dewey James rather prided herself on her dancing ability, but she concealed her annoyance with the aplomb of a diplomat. She reflected philosophically that it was probably all a part of the Norman Fox Technique—no point in telling people they don't need dancing lessons, she reasoned, if your livelihood depends on selling them.

"Yes, yes—'Those move easiest who have learned to dance,' they say," replied Dewey inconsequentially.

"That's a very nice saying. Mind if I borrow it? We're thinking of putting together a new logo," said Norman Fox.

1

"Well—it's not exactly mine to give away, you know," replied Dewey demurely.

"Uh-oh. I guess somebody used it before, huh?"

"Yes—but a very long time ago. I shouldn't think Mr. Pope will hear about your new logo."

"That's great. How did it go? 'You move easier if you learn to dance.' Nice. I like that." He nodded approval at this butchery of the great epigrammatist's phrase and turned his attention once more to the dance lesson. "Now: in tempo, one and two and three and four."

Dewey listened distractedly and looked around over Fox's shoulder at the depressing little studio. There were about eight other couples in the room, of all ages, sizes, and abilities; most looked as though they might prefer to face the firing squad at dawn than be forced to return to this stuffy little room, with its mirrored walls and strangely empty atmosphere. A banner of crepe paper dangled sadly from the ceiling; on a wall, a flimsy-looking poster declared that this week was National Ballroom Dance Week. As she whirled by in the reptilian clasp of Mr. Norman Fox, Dewey looked with amusement at the poster. "Dewey, old gal," she thought to herself, "you are living a bit of history."

In a far corner stood a lone, dilapidated loudspeaker, from whose murky depths came the painfully distorted sounds of a slow fox trot. The emerging noise was so grainy that the pupils and instructors alike had difficulty hearing the music; Dewey wondered briefly if it was all part of some diabolical master plan to throw one off, to convince petitioners at the altar of Terpsichore that they did, indeed, need the advice and encouragement of the In-Time School of Ballroom Dance. What on earth was she doing here? This was no place for Dewey James, a cheerful and intelligent widow who already knew how to waltz. It was all George's doing.

Norman Fox droned on about basic figures, extolling the liberating pulses of the merengue and the samba; Dewey pretended to listen as she studied the couples around her. She watched in mild irritation as her old friend George Farnham sailed by, sanguine in the generous embrace of a dark-haired, good-looking instructor called Delphine. George, at any rate, was having a good time.

As Norman Fox drew Dewey closer, she tensed, trying to remain politely in control of the distance between herself and this strangely repellent young man. She looked briefly into his pockmarked face. His eyes were an unsettling shade of brownish-yellow, and his strawlike auburn hair seemed to be shellacked down over his brow. He looked wizened, although he couldn't have been older than thirty-two or -three. There was something decidedly deathlike about him, thought Dewey, noting his strange pallor and waxy complexion. She stiffened her elbows. Why would anyone want to dance with him?

Norman Fox sensed her aversion but misconstrued its cause; in a tone of cloying omniscience he addressed himself to her reluctance. "Just relax," he said, moving in still closer. "You say you're a librarian?"

"Semiretired," said Dewey.

"Well, even librarians can kick up their heels. Soon you'll learn to enjoy being in the arms of a man." He smiled meaningfully down at her. With a huge effort of will Dewey forced herself to relax. She wasn't certain how much more of this she would be able to tolerate.

"*Much* better," said Norman Fox. "There we are."

He smiled at her again. "That's wonderful. Doesn't it make you feel special, to have this new experience? And dancing *will* improve your social life."

As Dewey fumbled for a suitable response, the music mercifully came to an end. A professional look of disappointment arrived on Norman Fox's face. "I'm afraid our little *pas de deux* is finished—for now. Duty calls." He nodded in the direction of the other dancers. "I'll return you to your partner—if you'll promise to dance with me again."

He unhanded her and bowed slightly, then greased his way across the shining hardwood floor. Dewey gave a slight shudder as the man headed for a pretty young woman who was struggling to keep a gangly youth moving in tempo.

"Now—that wasn't so bad, was it?" asked a friendly and familiar voice.

Dewey looked up into the sparkling eyes of her old friend and boon companion, George Farnham. She grimaced. "Never again, George," said Dewey in a deep whisper. "He really ought to be a mortician—he made me feel just like a corpse. How was Delphine? You seemed to be enjoying yourself."

"All in a good cause, my dear," said Farnham with a mischievous look. The music started up again, and he took her into his arms for an inexpert but lively two-step. "Just imagine how we'll show them all at the Homecoming Dance Contest. Only four days to go—hoho!" He beamed at Dewey.

George Farnham was a sturdy and energetic man, still handsome despite his gray hair. Most of the women Dewey's age would welcome him as a dance partner—and so, too, would some of the younger ones. George had a lot of style, Dewey had to admit. And if she hadn't ruled out the possibility of romance, he was just the type of man she might have gone for, the second time around.

"You're a perfectly marvelous dancer, George. You don't need these people." She gestured vaguely around with her head. "All you need is practice." She picked up her steps to match his.

"And what better place to practice? For all its charms, our little town of Hamilton isn't exactly overrun with nightclubs." He spun Dewey out and brought her back to him smoothly. "I do appreciate your willingness to partner me, my dear. After this evening's lesson I'll be as smooth as Fred Astaire."

Dewey scowled. "George, these people are very shady. If you're not careful, they'll have you signing away your life's savings for private lessons."

The In-Time School of Ballroom Dance was infamous. Several years ago the attorney general had threatened to revoke the school's license, citing rampant fraud in its curious contracts with unsuspecting hoofers. The owner had gone off to the Calvert Prison for a brief stretch; after his sentence was completed, he had returned to town and sold his house and his business. Naturally, townsfolk had referred to the place, ever since, as "Doin' Time." But so far, under the new management, there had been no hint of a misdemeanor, let alone felony.

"I doubt they'll be up to their old tricks any time soon. New owners and everything," replied Farnham. "Besides, the attorney general and I were at law school together forty years ago—a fact I made clear before I paid for this evening's little dip and swing."

"My—you are a clever one, George." Dewey James grinned at her old friend, her blue eyes shining with amusement. She tossed her silvery locks back in a youthful gesture.

"I'm so glad you think I'm clever." He spun Dewey out once more and brought her back to his arms just as the song ended.

The dancers stopped, looked about awkwardly, and then offered up a thin and unconvincing spurt of applause as Norman Fox moved to the center of the room. He glanced sorrowfully at his watch, clasped his hands together, and beamed on them in an attitude of proud joy. "People, you were *wonderful*," he oozed. "Simply marvelous. Alas, our time is up for the evening. We only had time for the basics in this specially priced group lesson. But Delphine and I have made extensive individual evaluations of your skills." He consulted a clipboard.

"Do you think he actually took notes?" Dewey whispered incredulously.

"Nah." Farnham shook his head. "All part of the act. Now he'll tell us we need more lessons."

On cue, Norman Fox went on. "I sense there is some natural ability here, but everyone is a little rusty. What you need is practice, plus the attention of a skilled dance instructor who can isolate any little trouble spots. Before long you'll be ready for one of those *romantic* old-fashioned steamboat cruises on the river. Or—who knows? A marvelous trip to Atlantic City! And if you act now, we have been authorized to offer you a very special, one-time-only discount of fifteen percent on *any* combination of private, one-to-one lessons." Dewey shuddered at the thought.

"Now," Fox went on, "if you'll just form a line, we'll get you all signed up with Delphine for your next lesson."

Delphine smiled warmly at George and, waving her clipboard invitingly, headed straight for him. But before she had managed to cross the room to where he and Dewey were standing, they had snatched up their belongings and hastened away.

2

"WHEW! THAT WAS a narrow one, eh, my dear?" George chuckled and took Dewey's arm as they headed up the pavement. "Watch your step here." He glanced up at the building next to the In-Time School. "New offices, I think, in the old mortar factory."

"Well," said Dewey uncertainly as she looked at the construction site, "I suppose it's a good thing that there's any construction at all down here."

It was a beautiful spring evening, and they strolled contentedly up the narrow little sidewalk, lined with nineteenth-century stone town houses. Hamilton, Dewey often thought, looked its best in the softening glow of evening. They passed a few shops, asleep for the night, and turned right up a steep hill, away from the river and toward the center of town.

"Anyhow, with a lesson under our belt, we'll be a shoe-in for the competition on Saturday night," George went on, taking a quick furtive look over his shoulder. "But let's keep this evening our little secret, eh?"

Dewey laughed. "Honestly, George, you are too much. There is no earthly reason to keep it a secret."

"Well—I'd rather people thought, when we win the dance contest on Saturday night, that it was spontaneous. You know—God-given talent and all that. Promise?"

"All right, if you insist. But it's dishonest. Anyway, George, I don't see what you thought we might get out of those people."

"I was hoping to learn the tango," replied George simply, with a smile.

"The *tango*? George, please." Dewey stopped in her tracks and fixed him with a look. "You don't think I'd tango with you at the Homecoming, do you? Honestly. You're letting all this hoopla about Jenny Riley's 'Tango Desperado' go to your head." She laughed. "Maybe Jenny will teach you to tango when she comes to town."

"No such luck." He smiled, his brow crinkling good-naturedly. "Unless, Dewey, as chief beneficiary of the Hamilton Homecoming, you can pull a few strings."

"Well, you're the chairman, George. Besides—I'm not the chief beneficiary. The library is."

"One and the same, eh, my dear?"

"If you choose to forget that I'm semiretired," replied Dewey with a smile.

In truth, Dewey was inclined to forget this fact herself. For more than thirty years she had presided over the Hamilton Free Library. An untrammeled spirit with an energetic intelligence, she had managed to turn the little place into a hot spot of the town's enthusiasms. But a few years ago, shortly after the death of her husband, Brendan, Dewey had reluctantly decided to relinquish her full-time responsibilities.

Unfortunately, Tom Campbell—the promising young man who had been hired to replace her—was a rather pathetic example of too much erudition grafted onto too little heart. Tom seemed to feel that his degree from a famous eastern university had somehow anointed him the town's chief intellectual, and he was tiresomely inclined to show off his scant knowledge. Dewey often felt herself obliged to step in and set things back on the course she approved. Although her official duties were now rather narrowly defined, she kept a hand in. She had given up the title of librarian, but she probably never would let go her authority.

"I can easily forget that, my dear," replied Farnham indulgently. "You have spent every day this week knee-deep in books. You even missed Tom's speech to the committee this afternoon on the need for a cultural dimension to the Homecoming."

"Oh, good heavens. What on earth could he mean? It's just a party to raise money. And to welcome home a few successful Hamiltonians."

"That's what I told him. Well, what I actually said was that he ought to find an audience at Hodgkins Funeral Parlor."

"George!" Dewey laughed. "He's rather sensitive, you know, under all that balderdash. Did you hurt his feelings?"

"Just a little. But he didn't stay long at the meeting—had to rush back to the library. He seemed a little worried about what you might do there, left to your own devices." George grinned fiendishly.

"Yes—well, Tom is in over his head, just at the moment. He so desperately wants to improve business that he's dreamed up a direct-mail campaign."

"Great Scott! I've never heard anything so absurd. Do you think there's a soul in Hamilton who doesn't know all about the library?"

Dewey chuckled. "It is rather silly, I agree. But I try to humor him. And at least, if he's doing that, he's not meddling with the collection."

"Very sound management practice, my dear. Well— since you missed this afternoon's meeting, you haven't heard the latest on the weekend's festivities. It seems that Jenny Riley is quite the crowd-pleaser: Susan Miles reports that the dinner and show are sold out. And there are thirty couples entered in the dance competition."

"Oh, that is wonderful news. I do hope we raise enough money to buy that new computer." Dewey was very gratified. Even if people in town weren't making their contributions directly to the Computer Fund, it was good to have such support.

"I heard she's really something when she dances," George added with an admiring sigh.

"Who—Jenny? Well, naturally, George. You don't get to have your own show on Broadway without being—well, *something*, at the very least," replied Dewey with a laugh. "But we'll see soon enough for ourselves."

Twelve years ago young Jenny Riley had packed her bags and moved to New York, accompanied by her high-school sweetheart, Tommy Jones. Both were aiming for great things. No one in town had been surprised, really, for Jenny had always been glamorous, had always dreamed of a career on the stage. And Tommy Jones planned to be a great writer.

Dewey had always had a bit of a soft spot for Tommy Jones, despite his reputation as a troublemaker, for he had been a frequent visitor to the library. She had thought his youthful devotion to Jenny was remarkable; he was constantly memorizing great love poems, reciting them softly to himself over the course of long afternoons. Even so, Dewey had been surprised when he gave up a university scholarship to go with Jenny to New York. And the news had come as a terrible blow to his parents.

Jenny, after several years of indifferent progress in modern dance, had suddenly and quite remarkably captured the attention of Alejandro Ponseca, a handsome and powerful dancer with a solid reputation in the theater. Together they had conceived and staged *Tentación!*—a lively amalgam of stylish and sexy dances from Argentina. The show had been a smash, running for two years at a small Broadway theater, and Jenny Riley had become a legend in her hometown.

But somewhere along the line, as Jenny was moving steadily toward success and fame, Tommy Jones had derailed. Eventually the word had come back to Hamilton that he had suffered a breakdown. No one knew, really, what had happened between them; just that it was over. Tommy was sick, and Jenny was a star. The last Dewey had heard of Tommy was that he was being cared for in a hospital in upstate New York.

Suddenly Dewey's mind was filled with an image of Tommy Jones—eager, skinny, enthusiastic, always trying to buck the system. Dewey rather admired people who gave the status quo a run for its money. "Do you know, George, I always thought it was so sad about Tommy."

"Never liked him myself." They had reached Laura's Wholly Natural Delites, where an after-dinner line had already begun to form. "How about an ice cream?"

Dewey wrinkled her brow. "What do you mean, you never liked him? I doubt you ever met him, George." George pushed open the door for her.

As they surveyed the list of tonight's offerings—just four homemade flavors, all guaranteed to be perfect—Dewey pursued the topic of Tommy Jones. "He wasn't a bad boy, George. A little willful, I'll grant you—but a great reader. He used to come to the library nearly every day."

"To read what—*The Great Ax Murderers of History*?"

"Don't be daft, George. He wasn't violent. Just—unusual. But rather a good writer, as I recall. He showed me one or two of his efforts. Short stories. I thought he had tremendous talent."

"Well, all I can say is that it didn't surprise anyone to hear that he had gone off his rocker. What will you have?"

"Vanilla. I think you're heartless, George."

"Sprinkles?" Dewey shook her head. "Two vanilla cones, please," said George to the girl behind the counter. "One with sprinkles. I'm not heartless, Dewey. Just think he was a bad egg, that boy. Had funny ideas about things."

"Good heavens, George! I've never heard you so full of small-town prejudice! What ever gave you that idea? Or, should I say, who put it into your mind?" George paid for the ice cream, and they stepped out once more into the warm spring air. George ignored her question. "Jack Riley, no doubt," pursued Dewey, looking darkly at her friend.

"Never known Jack to exaggerate," George replied at last, licking complacently at his ice cream.

"Come now, George. Fathers are notoriously biased about their daughters' beaux. Brendan used to give Grace's dates the third degree when she was a young girl."

"I don't suppose you let them off easy yourself, my dear."

"A mother is different." Dewey waved her ice cream

cone vaguely, indicating the whole world of mothers out there. "Anyway, you don't know Tommy. He was a very sensitive child, George, and rather highly strung, but there was nothing actually *wrong* with him in the old days."

"Well, my dear. I suppose I should trust your opinion of the boy. I certainly hope Jenny has come to terms with that business. I saw Mildred Jones in the grocery store yesterday, and she is none too pleased at the triumphant return of the great Miss Jenny Riley."

While Dewey and George were occupied with their ice cream, Delphine stepped into the small office at the In-Time School of Ballroom Dance and closed the door quietly behind her. In the yellowish light of the office she looked every minute of her thirty-nine years. There were heavy bluish-gray circles under her eyes, and the thick Pan-Cake makeup on her cheeks and forehead had begun to clot with perspiration.

She leaned up against the plywood door in a mock-provocative pose. "Well? How did we do, Killer?"

Norman Fox looked up from his papers and frowned at her. "I told you not to call me that." He consulted a piece of paper before him and grinned a jagged grin, his thin lips taut. "Six live ones tonight."

Delphine shook back her thick dark hair and pulled up a tattered-looking vinyl chair. "You nearly blew it with old Mrs. James, Norm."

"What do you mean, I nearly blew it?"

"I heard you schmoozing on about 'the arms of a man.' That old line hasn't worked for years. And I doubt if it ever would have worked on Dewey James, even if it wasn't the tiredest old horse in your stable. She doesn't fall for things."

"She didn't strike me as any too swift. Looked pretty out to lunch, if you ask me. Talked about the Pope or something. I can usually work wonders with the old bats, you know that."

Delphine leaned in and studied Fox's face carefully. "She's a smart old cookie. You better watch your step with her—and don't try any of your famous sales techniques. Her husband used to be the head cop in this dump, when he was alive. And now that he's dead, she hangs around with his deputy. Thinks she's a detective or something. And her boyfriend is a lawyer. So you better watch your step, Ki—Norm."

"Yeah, well, who wants to push an old bag like that around, anyway. Not me, thanks." He reached around and pulled open a small file cabinet and put the evening's paperwork away. "Makes me wonder why I ever came out here, people like that."

"Yeah, well we both know why you came out here."

"What's that supposed to mean?" Fox glared at her.

"Well, it's pretty easy pickings, right, Norm? And cheap to live here. And nobody knows you."

"You're full of it."

"So you keep telling me." Delphine narrowed her eyes and watched him carefully. "But you never did tell me why you left New York to manage some dumb dancing school in the sticks."

"None of your business. Your business is to sign up customers."

Delphine let it go. "Well? Tell me about tonight's pigeons, Baryshnikov."

Fox ignored her sarcasm. "Three for group lessons and three for private." He slammed the drawer shut and glowered at Delphine. "Ought to keep you in cheap red wine for a while, toots. You got nothing to complain about. Only two of 'em were yours."

"Men are always harder." Delphine kicked back in the chair and put her feet up on the edge of the desk. "But after the men in this town get a load of Jenny Riley, they'll be knocking down the door at this place. You watch."

Norman Fox made no reply. He fixed his gaze carefully on the far wall, narrowing his eyes.

Delphine watched him with interest. "Something gets you about her, right?" she asked at last.

"What?" Norman Fox stared at her. "No, nothing gets

me about her. Surprised she's performing in this rinky-dink town, that's all."

"Yeah, well you can bet it's all a big PR job. Something her agent is making her do. Small-town star returns to her roots, charms the yokels." Delphine lowered her feet to the floor, still watching Fox carefully. "She was the prom queen at Hamilton High. Wore the crown and everything. Or didn't she ever tell you?"

"Tell me? Whaddya mean, tell me? I never met her."

"Come off it, Norm. You go all weird every time anyone mentions her name. I think you have a thing for her. God, you danced in New York for years. What happened? She step on your toes?"

He shook his head. "She's big time. I was strictly small time. I never made it out of the East Village, except to ride the bus to Jersey."

"Well, maybe you should meet her. Maybe her devoted Alejandro needs a vacation or something. And you can't do a tango by your little old lonesome. Doesn't have the same effect." Delphine leaned heavily across the desk and gave him a kittenish look. "Why don't you offer yourself, in the service of Art?"

"Leave me alone, will you?" Norman Fox stood up abruptly and headed for the door. "And don't go blabbing all over town that I used to know her when. That's a lie."

He departed. Delphine sat thoughtfully for a few moments, watching his figure retreat down the hallway toward the front door. Then she gathered up her jacket and bag, locked the office door, and headed for her small apartment down in the old mill district by the river, where two disreputable tomcats awaited her solitary return.

3

PREPARATIONS FOR THE Hamilton Homecoming were in full swing, and it seemed that nearly everyone in town was involved, in one way or another. The Homecoming would be, without doubt, the biggest party that this little town had thrown in many a year.

It was Dewey's friend Susan Miles who had originally come up with the idea. One day as she sat under the bonnet of a large hair dryer at the Tidal Wave Beauty Shop, flipping through the pages of *StarLife* magazine, she had been surprised to read that Gloria Peters, a Hamilton native, was slated to star in the TV miniseries *Blind Devotion*. The discovery led Susan and the other customers into a discussion of other Hamiltonians who had moved on to fame and fortune. Susan had proposed, half facetiously, that the town invite them all home again to be lionized.

To Susan's surprise, the idea had spread like wildfire, and before long the town council had taken up the matter. The fund-raising potential of such an event was quickly apparent to the canny minds of the council; and there were several good causes in town (Dewey's beloved library among them) that were feeling the pinch. In the Homecoming, Hamilton had found a way out of a tiresome budgetary problem.

It took little time to get the whole thing in motion. Unfortunately, Gloria Peters—who had been, in a sense, the festival's inspiration—couldn't make it to the Homecoming; she pleaded a tight production schedule for her new TV movie, *Snake Eyes in Reno*. But Hamilton had spawned quite a few successful sons and daughters, now living in

15

far-flung cities and towns, and some had been enthusiastic in their response.

Naturally, those former Hamiltonians who had felt the call of political life had been eager to attend. But there were others as well: The head of a large corporation had written to say that he might be free for breakfast; a writer whose star was fading behind a thick alcoholic fog was hoping to cover the event for a regional travel magazine; and a well-known senior circuit golf pro, who had sprained his wrist badly, had offered to give charity lessons on the public course.

But above all there was Jenny Riley.

She was a phenomenon. A sleepy-looking beauty with magnificent stage presence, she had captivated the minds and hearts of theatergoers in New York with her offbeat dance extravaganza. It had helped to have, in Alejandro Ponseca, a most remarkable partner—handsome, suave, and confident. He was mature enough to recognize Jenny's power over audiences, and to use it wisely; always deferential, always adoring, he was idealized by women and envied by men. It suited him well, the role of the lover. Audiences ate it up. He had played it exactly right.

Invitations to the Homecoming had gone out to several dozen less famous ex-Hamiltonians, and the response had been tremendously encouraging. Every room at the charmingly down-at-the-heel Hamilton Inn had been booked for weeks, and business was nearly as brisk at the seedy but congenial Canalside Lodge.

The grand celebration, now but four days away, would open with a River Festival, complete with boat rides, a trolling contest, and speeches. (A United States senator, up for reelection, was going to kick it off. Sid Smith, a local fisherman, happened to have a new rowboat; Senator Davidson had grandly offered to christen it.) After the lunch of fresh fish and baked potatoes, the townspeople would make their way to the Hamilton High football stadium for a bluegrass concert. But the high point would be the evening's festivities. This multitiered extravaganza had everyone in town breathless with anticipation.

The Straw Hat Supper Dance was scheduled for early Saturday evening. George Farnham, who was not only town council president but also chairman of the Homecoming Committee, would judge the hats, scoring them for inventiveness, artistry, and practicality; the winner would receive dinner for two at Panella's Italian Villa. (In consequence, there had been a run on ribbons and rickrack at Nellie's Five and Dime—for Panella's was the best spot in town.) After the hats were judged, there would be a dance competition, with Nils Reichart, proprietor of the Seven Locks Tavern, presiding as judge and jury.

But the evening would reach its zenith when Jenny Riley and Alejandro Ponseca danced the Tango Desperado—a half hour of the hottest numbers from their hit show, *Tentación!*

Not everyone in town was pleased at the prospect of the glamorous young dancer's return. As George Farnham had mentioned to Dewey, Mildred Jones, mother of Tommy, was unnerved at the thought of seeing Jenny Riley once more. She had never liked Jenny; and when her precious Tommy had taken off for New York, throwing away all his chances in the world, she had brooded in deepest misery, as only a mother can brood.

Jenny Riley, Mildred would always agree, was a charming and beautiful girl. But Jenny Riley had room in her heart for only Jenny Riley. Tommy had been madly infatuated with her, but Mildred had known, even then, that the romance would lead to disaster. Tommy was unpredictable and sensitive. He deserved the true affection of a good, strong, kindly woman, a woman with his best interests at heart. A woman like Mildred herself. A mother knows these things.

As she waited in line at the checkout counter at Freddie's Grocery on the Wednesday before the Homecoming, Mildred Jones was rehearsing in her mind her approach to the coming occasion. She knew that it would be rude to ignore Jenny—and that, given the town's mood, any attempt to snub the young woman would be greeted with misguided attempts at kindness, or else with pity. Pity was the last thing that Mildred Jones wanted. In fact, as her plan began to take shape, she rather hoped that people had forgotten all about Tommy and Jenny. It wouldn't do to have public attention focused on Tommy's mother this weekend. She wanted to get back a little of her own from the headstrong and selfish young woman who had ruined Tommy's life. It was just a question of how to go about it.

Fortunately, Mildred Jones was well placed. Everyone in town knew that Jenny Riley had declined her father's invitation to stay with him. (Some considered it a scandal, and others thought Jenny was behaving with great tact. Jack Riley, after all, was not a wealthy man; his little apartment, down in the canal district, was cramped and dark, and there really wasn't room.) So Jenny had booked two rooms at the Hamilton Inn. This Mildred Jones knew—two rooms, one for Jenny herself and one for her partner, that Latin type, Carlos or Pepe or whatever his name was. Mildred Jones knew just which rooms, even. Mildred Jones was the desk clerk at the Hamilton Inn.

It had taken her several days and nights of long thought, but at last Mildred Jones had her plan. She knew that she could make it work; it was all a question of timing. The mechanics of it were simple enough, and in fact, it was she who had started the ball rolling. Now all she had to do was bide her time until that young lady made her splendid entrance into the lives she had left behind. Then Miss Jenny Riley would get a taste of what it was like to be left with nothing but broken dreams.

4

AT NOON ON the Thursday before the Homecoming, the committee was having one last dust-up to prepare for the big event. They met in George Farnham's fourth-floor office in the old Grain Merchants Exchange Building—an enormous Greek Revival temple to commerce that recalled the town's glory days at the hub of the great railways linking the East Coast to the river traffic and the territories of the West.

In attendance were Nils Reichart; Susan Miles, whose brainchild the Homecoming had been; Dewey James; the new librarian, Tom Campbell; and George himself.

The little group had reached a tense and unfriendly stalemate. Against the express wishes of the committee, Tom Campbell had made one last desperate attempt to raise the tone of the evening's festivities: He had asked a notoriously dull professor of anthropology to give a lecture during the Straw Hat Supper. Professor Needham Renfrew was to regale them all on "The Importance of Festivals in Society." Campbell knew he had gone too far; but he hoped it was now too late to cancel.

But Campbell had sadly misjudged the committee's opinion of social anthropology, Professor Renfrew, and lectures in general. All the other members were solidly opposed, and Nils Reichart had insisted that the invitation be rescinded.

"But one can't possibly uninvite the man, Nils. That would be unthinkably rude. Besides—he's a professor at my own alma mater. It would distress me more than I can say—and just imagine how it will reflect on the limited

scope of the inhabitants of this town. I must insist that we
allow the professor to give us the benefit of his insights and
experience."

"No, Tom," said George Farnham, shaking his head
firmly. "I'm sorry—the Homecoming is a festival, not a
seminar. We don't want some loudmouthed academic chasing everyone away with the promise of improving their
minds. We're trying to make money, for Pete's sake—not
find a cure for insomnia."

Campbell looked pityingly at Farnham, an expression of
resigned patience on his face. He let out air slowly from
between compressed lips and shook his head. "I think you'll
find, er—George—that the people of Hamilton are not
nearly so intellectually backward as you make out. I'm sure
there are a great number who would find the lecture
stimulating. And it would certainly elevate the tone of the
thing above the level of a common barn dance."

"I like barn dances," said Susan Miles, a good-looking
mother of two glorious little girls, and a great friend of
Dewey's. "The commoner the better. I bet you would, too,
Tom, if you'd give it half a try. Mary Barstow, you know,
would love a chance to do-si-do with you," she added
fiendishly. Mary Barstow was a dental hygienist with a
well-known eye for the men. Susan knew well that Mary
would be extremely unlikely to give Tom Campbell the time
of day; but the idea was amusing.

Campbell looked scandalized. "Good heavens!" He
turned slightly pink. "I certainly will not do-si-do."

"Give it up, Tom," encouraged Nils Reichart. He was a
big, handsome, burly man with curly red hair and bright red
cheeks. He was a singularly civic-minded barkeep, and well
known as a *bon vivant rustique*. "Nobody in this room—
especially George—thinks people in Hamilton are dumb.
Well, maybe there's one exception."

"I promise you, Nils, that you, too, would find the
professor's lecture most stimulating. And he has had a great
many occasions to give it, you know; he's refined it, made
it—er—accessible to the layman."

Susan Miles leaned over and whispered conspiratorially to Dewey. "Missionary among the savages," she said.

Dewey James nodded. "The Bright Man's Burden," Dewey whispered back. Dewey was losing patience with Tom Campbell.

"It's a unique opportunity to expand the depth and breadth of this affair," protested Campbell, removing his spectacles and polishing them carefully. "You surely don't mean to pass it up? Dr. Renfrew is the most noted, most highly respected authority on the topic—"

"Tom," interposed Dewey in dangerously meek tones. "I don't think you're going to win this one. But I'm sure everyone would be charmed to meet Dr. Renfrew—it's been many years since he paid a visit to his humble hometown. Why don't we offer him tea at the library on Friday afternoon and invite people to come round? A little open house, the kind of thing they do in Senior Common Rooms at Oxford." Tom Campbell's face grew instantly hopeful. "We could even serve sherry, if you think we dare," added Dewey with a gleam.

A sense of grateful relief passed through the assembled committee members. George smiled broadly. "Terrific idea, Dewey. I'm sure that there will be plenty of people who might like to hear what Dr. Renfrew has to say—in more intimate surroundings. Topic's really much more suited to a seminar, anyway, wouldn't you agree, Tom? Not squeezed in between the macaroni salad and the fox-trot."

Tom Campbell knew when he was beaten, but at least he had forged a small link in the chain that he hoped would someday make Hamilton a leading cultural and intellectual center. He nodded somberly and pulled at his chin. "I can see that—yes, I can, indeed. Fine suggestion, Mrs. James. In fact, I'll pop over right now to call Renfrew, see what kinds of materials he might need, get things in motion. Do you think we can locate a slide projector anywhere, Mrs. James?"

"You're welcome to use mine," offered Reichart with a wink at Dewey.

"Oh, thank you. That's most generous," said Campbell,

rising. "Well, now, I'd better get going on all of this—if the committee will excuse me?"

The committee would, and happily. With a feeling of mutual relief, the members turned their attention to the truly important matters before them: the size limits on hats eligible for the Grand Prize; Saturday night's dessert; and the question of whether to use bottled root beer or a keg of Sam Duncan's Homemade Sarsaparilla for refreshments at the River Festival.

It was well known in Hamilton that Rob Jensen, proprietor of Jensen's Feed & Grain, liked to spend his Thursday afternoons away from his store. Nobody begrudged him this little luxury, because the store was open early and late every other day of the week. Some Thursdays Jensen called on his big customers, assessing their needs and nodding sympathetically as they poured out stories of lame horses or withering crops. On other Thursdays he sometimes disappeared on solitary fishing expeditions. Occasionally, if it rained, Rob Jensen would spend his Thursdays shooting pool in the cool darkness of the back room at the Seven Locks Tavern. Jensen's customers were used to his schedule, and as a rule no one came by the store unless there was some kind of emergency. Young Amy Freeman filled in on Thursdays, but she was only there to answer the phone and handle a few light chores.

This Thursday was typical. Amy had been at the store since three o'clock, all alone. By four forty-five, with her chores completed, she was thoroughly bored; but her father wouldn't be coming by to collect her till closing time—five-thirty. Rob had told her she could use the telephone after five o'clock, so on this Thursday—like every Thursday—Amy Freeman was on the phone with her best friend at five o'clock sharp. Such were the well-established rhythms of life in Hamilton.

"Well, of course we're going to enter the contest," Amy was saying into the telephone. "I don't think we've got too much in the way of competition, either." She looked up in distracted surprise as the shop door opened. "Hang on, Helene." She covered the mouthpiece. "Yeah?"

"It's my roses. Aphids. I wondered if you have something for them."

Amy Freeman pointed vaguely toward a far wall. "Over there. Rob always looks in the big blue book first, to see what kind of stuff to use. Then on that rack." She went back to her conversation. "So anyway, who else would there be? I mean, Phil and I have been dating for like six months, and we go dancing at the Youth Center every Saturday. So who could beat us?" She listened, examining her nails. "Nah, I doubt it. Hang on again." She put the telephone down briefly as the customer returned. "This should do it, I guess," she said abstractedly, ringing up the sale. "Nine eighty-seven." She took the proffered ten and gave change. "Wanna bag?"

"No, thank you," replied the customer, picking up the small canister and heading for the door.

Amy Freeman took up the phone again. "Sorry. I actually had a customer. Unreal. So anyway, are you bringing Doug or what?" she asked into the telephone, as the door to Jensen's Feed & Grain swung gently closed.

"You must tell me what is the matter. I know—you have had some kind of letter. I am right, yes? And it frightens you. Jenny, you must share this burden with me," said Alejandro Ponseca, taking Jenny Riley firmly in his arms.

"Oh, stop being so dramatic, Alejandro. Honestly. It's nothing." Jenny freed herself from his grip and shook back her black hair, a look of irritation in her deep blue eyes. "Will you quit being so—so—"

"So much the Latin lover?" Alejandro Ponseca smiled softly and gently reached out to brush a dark curl out of Jenny's eyes. "All right, my dear." He shrugged. "I have asked, and you have answered—or rather, you have chosen not to answer me. But I—your partner, who knows every move you make, who can see from the set of your chin what kind of mood you are in—I am surprised at you. That you should consider to make such a childish attempt to hide from me your fears."

Jenny moved across the room and stepped out through French doors onto the tiny terrace of her apartment. Before her the lights of Manhattan winked and shone in the darkness. Ponseca followed, looking at his partner curiously.

She leaned up against the brick retaining wall and stared. Seventeen stories down the traffic whizzed by, the noise rebounding strangely off the sides of the buildings across the street. "This is such a funny place to have ended up," she said softly.

"What is this—ended?" he asked her. "My dearest Jenny, your life is before you. You are just beginning." He put an arm around her shoulders and stared with her out at the lights of the city.

"I used to be able to see the Empire State Building at night. Before they put up that thing." She pointed off toward an ungainly tower, half built and unlighted, that thrust itself intrusively into the skyline. "It's condos."

"Yes, of that I am certain," said Ponseca, his voice grave. He turned her toward him. "What is it you are frightened of, in this famous hometown of yours?"

"Haven't you ever been frightened of going home again?"

Ponseca laughed. "Yes—but of course, when I go home, I may have to face a wrathful husband, or an affronted father or brother. Very different. And I am never afraid—as you are afraid now."

"It's nothing that I can't handle. Honestly, Alejandro. It's just so scary—the thought of being back among all those people from my childhood. I haven't seen my father since I left. What if he's disappointed in me?" She smiled.

Ponseca shook his head. "That would be too sad for your father, I think. But is that all?"

"That's all—all that's important, anyway. Anything else is my problem. Kind of a moment of truth for me."

"All right. But, as I am coming with you—don't you

think it would be smart to tell me what kind of trouble to expect for myself?"

Jenny laughed. "The only trouble you have to watch out for is from the ladies, Alejandro. As always. Now, go away and leave me in peace. I want to pack. I'll pick you up at eight-thirty, sharp."

Ponseca did as he was asked, and Jenny Riley packed her bags for her journey home.

5

"IN CERTAIN SOCIETIES, of course, festivals of thanks or of petition reached their climax of—of hilarity, if you will—in ritual human sacrifice." Professor Needham Renfrew blinked and coughed dryly, gazing vaguely at his little audience with an amused air. "You may look, if you like, to some of the early cultures of Central and South America. The Druids, too, were said to have required the death of one of their own number in the efficacious carrying out of certain religious rites—witness the Peat Bog Man, recently discovered perfectly preserved in an English bog, with the trappings of high Druidical priesthood about him."

Here Professor Renfrew permitted himself a small chuckle. He was a small, disheveled, unformed-looking man, with thinning curls and greasy lenses in his wire-rimmed spectacles. Dewey nodded back at him with a bright-eyed enthusiasm that she did not feel. There was something truly frightening about this man. And she didn't like the turn his lecture was taking: He had been talking now for fifteen minutes about ritual sacrifice as an adjunct to festivals in human history. The topic was certainly unwelcome, on the day before the Hamilton Homecoming.

At least the attendance at the lecture had turned out to be a success, pleasing Tom Campbell no end. Thirty people had made their way to the library on Friday evening to hear what Needham Renfrew had to say about festivals and society. Dewey looked around. George was there, of course, along with the rest of the Homecoming Committee members—she had been most firm about their attending.

26

But there was an interesting assortment of others here as well. Even Jenny Riley had come, bringing Alejandro Ponseca with her. She had arrived in town at lunchtime, amidst great fanfare, and she had seemed truly delighted to be home again.

Now most of the audience sat wide-eyed, their mouths slightly open—a perfect picture of surprise. Nobody had expected quite such a gruesome talk, here at the quiet little Hamilton Library.

Dewey supposed she oughtn't to have been surprised at the evening's turnout. Needham Renfrew was, after all, a fairly famous Hamiltonian; he had written several books on his subject, which had been well received in university press circles, and he had even once been invited to lecture a captive audience on a passenger liner making its way down the coast of Mexico. Dewey supposed it was natural for the townsfolk to be interested in what this homegrown intellectual had to say. Besides, the video store was closed—the owner was down with the flu.

"Of course, the desire to spill blood in this way is not dead in our society; merely muted," Renfrew was saying. "It expresses itself in other, more acceptable forms. But it hasn't died. Consider, if you will, 'The Lottery'—the short story by Shirley Jackson. The effectiveness of the tale lies in its absolute credibility. We know we ought to turn away in horror, but we are drawn in, fascinated. The impact is in the remarkable realism of the tale. There is no question that the mood persists in our towns to make some kind of sacrificial offering. We channel it—or we attempt to. Our own Thanksgiving, you may even say, retains a vestige of this primitive hopefulness, in *Meleagris gallopavo*—the unlucky turkey."

"Good heavens!" murmured Dewey to George. "This man is positively bloodthirsty!"

George nodded. "Look at the way he licks his lips," he replied.

"In other societies," Renfrew was saying, "a mythological or religious figure is sometimes called upon to be the centerpiece of the drama—as is true in certain of the Shiva festivals in southern India. The stand-in fulfills the requirements for appeasement, the lust for blood is satisfied, yet no human blood is actually spilt. And then of course there are the animal substitutes. Bearbaiting, bullfighting, a wide variety of guises under which murder—for we must call it that—is perpetrated." He smiled. "Perhaps Mr. Ponseca would be good enough to enlarge on the sport of bullfighting for us, a little later." He nodded toward Jenny's partner, who sat handsomely upright and kept his face politely still at this suggestion. "All these substitutes make for a much neater ritual, morally speaking—although who can say whether it has the same persuasive influence over the will of the god or gods in question?"

Renfrew paused dramatically and rubbed his hands together. In the audience no one stirred. Renfrew smiled thinly, and the light glinted off his spectacles, making his eyes ghostly circles. Suddenly the lights blinked and went out.

There was silence for a moment, then a confused chattering that grew louder and louder. Finally Dewey managed to make herself heard over the crowd. "Tom, the circuit breaker is right there. Right where you are standing. Open up the little door and flip the switches up."

"Er, what little door is that, Mrs. James?"

"Oh, honestly, Tom." Dewey groped in the darkness, stumbling through the little crowd toward Tom Campbell.

"That's all right, Mrs. James," came another voice. It was Alfred Scott, one of Dewey's neighbors. Thank heaven, thought Dewey.

"I've got it," said Scott. He felt for the small hasp and pulled the little metal door open. Within seconds the lights were restored.

Dewey gave Tom Campbell a withering look.

At the podium Needham Renfrew went on, almost without pausing. If he sensed the deep unease in the crowd before him, he didn't acknowledge it. Instead, he ran through a few more examples from modern popular authors, smiling a thin, dry smile as he talked. Finally, he began to wind down; the lecture was coming to its end.

"We know the need is there, to expiate, to cajole, to petition, and to appease," he said. "In all of our doings the desire to please a wrathful Providence persists—even here in Hamilton. We can't know, in our humble human brains, whether Providence is fooled by such easy substitutions. Perhaps, however, we shall know"—Renfrew smiled— "bye and bye. I thank you." He took a small, birdlike bow as the little audience, stunned, belatedly began to applaud.

Tom Campbell rose with alacrity to shake the professor's hand. Dewey hurried to take up her post behind the circulation desk, which today had been converted into a bar, and began to pour out the sherry and lemonade.

"Whew!" said Susan Miles to Dewey, hastening up to the counter. "Human sacrifice. That lecture gave me the creeps, Dewey. Do you think that business with the lights was an omen?" She rapped her knuckles meaningfully on the wooden surface of the circulation desk.

Dewey smiled at her friend. "Well, well—you are superstitious grown of late." She handed Susan a paper cup filled with sherry. "Drink this. You'll feel more like yourself. No, I think it was Providence begging that man to stop."

Susan shivered and took the cup. "Oooh! That's one of those subjects that I have always found frightening. You know?"

"Oh, yes indeed, I know. Don't think about it. I admit—it wasn't exactly the dry historical analysis I had anticipated." She looked around at the other audience members, who were slowly making their way to the circulation desk. "But anyway, we got quite a nice turnout for the affair. Hello, Mary. Hello, Alfred," said Dewey to some newcomers at her makeshift bar. "Care for some refreshment?"

Mary Royce, publisher of the Hamilton *Quill*, smiled at Dewey. She was a dark-haired beauty of impeccable manners and an orderly air that masked a deep-seated love of mischief. "Hi, Dewey. Yes, I could certainly use a drink after that grisly little seminar."

"I'll have some of that, too, if you please, Dewey," said

Alfred Scott, taking a cup. "That was not what I had expected tonight, somehow—a grim catalog of atrocities."

Mary accepted a cup of sherry. "Boy, I'll say. It reminded me of the ghost stories we used to tell each other in the dark at summer camp—you know, about the escaped murderer who's waiting in the basement until your parents go out. Sonny got the whole thing on tape." Dewey looked up and spotted Sonny Royce, Mary's husband, across the room. He was shooting a picture of Renfrew and Campbell before the podium.

"I think that man's got a fixation," put in Alfred Scott, a pale-eyed, soft-looking man in his early thirties. Scott had once been wealthy in his own right; he was one of those young men who, with just enough fortune behind them, manage to do nothing at all. He had made a stab, briefly, at being a literary agent; but the workload was oppressive, so he had married Abby Ambler, daughter of the richest family in town, and turned to writing. He nodded toward Renfrew. "Not the kind of thing we get up to here in Hamilton."

"I should hope not. Thank you, by the way, Alfred, for fixing the circuit-breaker. Tom, I'm afraid, hasn't your genius for electrical things."

"No problem," said Alfred Scott. "Glad to help out. If I fail as a writer, I guess I could always become an electrician. Better money, anyway. Say, Dewey—it's awfully good of you to offer to give me a book party next week."

"Oh, Alfred—well. You ought really to thank Tom Campbell, you know. It was his idea." Dewey didn't care much for Alfred, but was pleased that he had written a book. It was the only actual bit of work that Alfred was known to have done in his thirty-odd years. It was called *Blues*, and those in the know said it was a skillfully concocted thriller about a captain of the Coast Guard who uncovers a deadly Cuban plot to overthrow the United States government. The rumor in town was that Scott had been offered a fabulous advance by Harbison House, one of the great old New York publishers. "We can't wait to see it," Dewey added politely.

"Hah!" said Scott, downing his sherry in one gulp. "I

can't wait for you to read the part where the beautiful librarian falls in love with the gruff but handsome spy and decodes the secret documents."

"It sounds marvelous. Although where you got the notion for such a lively librarian, Alfred, I don't know." Dewey turned pink.

"What's that you say?" George Farnham stepped up to the counter and helped himself to sherry. "You were always twice as lively as anyone in town, Dewey," said George with a wink. "Why, if I didn't know better, I'd say that Alfred here had lifted his whole plot from the story of your life."

"Er—yes, quite so," replied Scott good-naturedly. "Hello, darling," he said as his wife, Abby, joined their little circle.

Abby Scott was a beautiful young woman, with golden curls and deep blue eyes. Dewey had a notion that everything wasn't quite right in the marriage, but as she regarded the couple this evening, she forced herself to restrain from speculation. "Don't ask him where he got his idea for the book," said Abby. "He hates boats, gets seasick at the drop of a hat. But Harbison House has offered him—"

"Yes, my dear," said Alfred Scott hastily. "Enough about me. Look, here comes Jenny."

Jenny Riley and Alejandro Ponseca made their way to the circulation desk. "Hiya, Mrs. James," said Jenny with a big smile.

"Goodness, Jenny," said Dewey warmly. She shook the young dancer's hand. "You look absolutely marvelous, my dear. It's wonderful of you to come for our little event."

"She would not have missed your party for the world, señora," put in Alejandro Ponseca handsomely. "Jenny has told me many wonderful things about your library."

"We are very pleased to have you here as well, Mr. Ponseca," said Dewey politely. "Will you have a glass of sherry?"

"Ahh. *Jerez*," he said, sounding gratified. "You are most cultivated and kind, señora." Dewey looked pleased. Alejandro Ponseca was, undeniably, a remarkably handsome and captivating young man. He lingered at the circulation desk, utterly at his ease, as Jenny made the rounds in the crowd.

"Well, now," said George Farnham heartily. "That was rather an interesting little talk, wouldn't you agree, everyone? I had no idea that human sacrifice was considered such an essential part of the festivities in small-town life. Wonder who we ought to offer up?"

"George, please, don't!" exclaimed Susan.

"Got to choose someone, Susan," said George ghoulishly. "Like Ko-Ko, you know. The Lord High Executioner."

"Yes, George, we know," said Dewey brightly. "I vote for the people who eat peppermint and puff it in your face."

"She's got a little list," chimed in Mary Royce.

"Hah!" exclaimed Alfred Scott. "I believe that fellow got to you all, didn't he? You're all as nervous as cats and whistling in the dark."

"It was kind of gruesome," admitted Abby Scott. "You're used to him, Alfred, because you read that book of his on capital punishment."

"Yes—toughened me up. But I'm surprised at you, George," said Scott. "I thought lawyers were accustomed to the dark side of human souls."

"Naturally, Alfred—the everyday dark side—cheating and stealing and doing down your friends—all in the course of business. But even lawyers cavil at cold-blooded killing, done right out in the open like that."

"That's right," agreed Sonny Royce, who had put away his camera and joined the little group at the circulation desk. He was a tall, bearded man, with a gentle manner, an intelligent look in his eye, and an air of perpetual bonhomie. "For that kind of thing you need a two-thirds vote in the Congress," he said mischievously. "Cheers."

"Cheers," replied George. "Got your dancing pumps ready, Sonny?"

Sonny Royce laughed and put an arm around his wife. "Well, now, George—tell me honestly. Has Mary been working on you?"

"Good heavens, no!" said George. "Can't imagine what you mean." He winked at Mary, who had indeed put him up to the question. Sonny's disinclination to dance irritated Mary Royce, who loved to kick up her heels. "But you know, without any competition, Dewey and I will walk away with the prize tomorrow night. Thought maybe you'd like to give us a run for our money." He smiled at Ponseca. "Fortunately, sir, you and Miss Riley will not be taking part in our little amateur hour. I'd hang up my pumps, of course, if you were."

"Oh, I wouldn't be too sure of your prize, George," put in Susan Miles. "I stopped by the committee room this afternoon. And do you know who has entered the contest?"

"No," said Mary Royce obligingly. "Do tell."

"The instructors from the In-Time School of Ballroom Dance!"

George choked on his sherry, and Dewey stifled a laugh. "You aren't serious, Susan?"

"Oh, yes. I doubt you even know them. A woman called Delphine something or other. And a man, her business partner."

"Delphine Charlotte," said Dewey as George glared at her. "I remember her from long ago." She gave George a wide-eyed, noncommittal look. "Oh, look, here's Professor Renfrew at last." She waved to Tom Campbell, who seemed not to want to let the professor out of his sight. "Tom!" she called. "Let poor Professor Renfrew have a drink. He must be parched."

"Thank you, Mrs. James," replied the little professor, making his way to the bar. "Mr. Campbell was just telling me how ably you assist him in running this fine little library."

The little group standing by the circulation desk sputtered together, and George began to speak, but Dewey cut him off neatly.

"Oh, was he?" she asked politely. "Well, that *is* handsome of him. Come and have a drink, Tom. It will take your mind off sacrificial lambs."

"Er—thank you, Mrs. James," said Tom Campbell,

detaching himself from Jenny Riley. "Well, now, how did everyone like the professor's little talk? Not too academic and dull, was it?"

There was an uncomfortable momentary silence, broken at last by George Farnham. "Hardly dull, good heavens, no!" he said. "A little bit on the frightening side, if you ask me."

"Just so, just so," concurred the professor with evident pleasure. "That little talk is intended to be somewhat electrifying. No good being complacent, you know. We live in very dark times, dark times." He nodded to the group and sipped gingerly at his sherry. "I have made rather a study of the cathartic effects of murder, especially the socially sanctioned killing that, historically, has accompanied festivals of all sorts. The yin and yang of it fascinates me: dark and light, joy and pain."

Susan Miles held her empty paper cup out to George Farnham, who obliged by filling it. Sonny Royce, interested, pressed on. "I suppose, Professor, that such studies as yours are rather common among your colleagues. That is to say—"

"Rather unusual, actually, Mr. Royce. I must admit it's a strange sideline of interest—but then, so much of our human history, or what is recorded of it, is precisely a roll call of murder." He beamed around at the little group. "When it's done for one person's gain, we call it a crime; but when it redounds to the benefit of all the survivors of the deed, we call it a sacrifice. I think, at heart, we are all Benthamites."

"But surely, Professor," put in Tom Campbell, eager to show that he understood what a Benthamite was, "you must agree that twentieth-century society has progressed beyond that kind of thing. We're not Picts or Celts or Druids anymore. This is America."

"Precisely so, my good man. And now you know why I have come to your little gathering." Renfrew smiled strangely, and Dewey began to feel uneasy. She didn't like this turn of the conversation. It was as though the professor sensed, in their silly town festival, an occasion for voicing his theories.

"Goodness, Professor," she interjected heartily. "It was very good of you to find time to attend our little Homecoming." Dewey stepped out from behind the circulation desk and, taking the professor's arm, led him off in the direction of the rare book collection. "It's been quite a while, hasn't it, since you left Hamilton? And I'm so glad you approve of the library—because we are lucky enough to be the beneficiaries of the money raised. Do let me show you around."

A sigh of relief went up among the little group left standing at the bar. George reached for the sherry. "Where'd you dig him up, Tom? He's like the ghost at the banquet."

"Yes, Tom, why on earth did you invite him to talk about ritual killing in our library?" Mary Royce was indignant. "He gives me the creeps, that man."

"I promised you it would be interesting," replied Campbell with one of his rare smiles. "Cheers."

6

DEWEY AWOKE THE next morning with a deep sense of unease. In spite of her cool-headed response to ghost stories and scare tactics in general, Professor Renfrew's lecture had alarmed her. There had been something frighteningly oracular in his delivery. Arriving home to her big old farmhouse long after dark, she had been immensely comforted by the presence of Isaiah, her faithful and predictable black labrador retriever. She had gone so far as to give the dog a piece of leftover sausage as a reward for being there; and she had permitted him to sleep indoors, telling herself that it looked like rain.

But even the presence of the snoring Isaiah on the hooked rug beside her bed hadn't been enough to ward off nightmares. She had dreamed of shadowy figures entering her house, waiting downstairs for her, their eyes hidden behind milky spectacles. As she watched, appalled, from the top of the staircase, they had danced around a large black hole in the floor, chanting in an impenetrable language. But Dewey knew what they were saying. They were calling out for blood. She had awakened herself at 3:00 A.M. with her own attempts to cry out; after that she slept fitfully until daybreak.

"Good heavens!" said Dewey aloud, waking for the last time that morning. "Isaiah?" She looked down at her dog, who yawned and stretched, then slowly blinked his eyes at her. "Isaiah!" He wagged his tail and rose stiffly, cold-nosing her outstretched hand. Dewey couldn't remember the last time she had had such a nightmare. The feeling of it was still with her; she knew it would persist until she had shaken it loose with some kind of activity. So as the sun rose over the gentle hillside to the east, Dewey donned her oldest clothes and, after giving Isaiah a big bowl of food, headed for a small, ramshackle red stable building behind her house.

The morning was cool and moist; it was still that time of the spring when early risers are glad of a heavy sweater or jacket. She swung open the stable door and greeted the surprised-looking chestnut mare within, giving her a hearty rub upon the nose. "Hello, my beautiful old Starbuck," said Dewey. The ancient mare let out a heavy snort of greeting. "You understand me tolerably well; and I converse with you at least four hours every day." The mare nuzzled Dewey's neck and stomped a foot.

Dewey fed Starbuck a small snack, then saddled her up and moved slowly off into the misty countryside. The rolling hills spread out before her; she crossed down through her own small pasture and over the downs of an adjoining farm. Then she followed a trail up a steep hill to a point where she could see for nearly ten miles, straight down through the river valley and across the river to the gentle farmland beyond the other bank.

Hamilton really was a beautiful place. Much of the countryside belonged, these days, to wealthy breeders of racehorses, and the vista before Dewey was lush green pastureland, genteelly punctuated with picturesque white post-and-rail fences. Toward the north, there were still a few working farms; and fifty or so miles beyond them was the sprawl of the state capital. Southward, downriver, lay the town of Hamilton proper. Here the terrain leveled out, and beyond was the confluence of two large rivers, the Boone and the Gunpowder. Dewey could make out the old mill buildings down by the Boone River; the last one in her line of sight, just before the river took a wide turn to the left, was George Farnham's house. This was where George had retreated some years ago, after his wife's death had made their old farmhouse intolerable to him; and he had

converted the mill lovingly and single-handedly into one of
the most beautiful and appealing dwellings in town.

Hamilton's prosperity was a thing of the past; but most of
its present-day inhabitants liked the status quo. There was
still enough light industry in the region to keep the population diverse and lively; and the "horse crowd," as Dewey
thought of them, had not lost the knack of being friends to
their neighbors. Occasionally the beauty of the spot, and the
relatively low price of land, tempted real-estate speculators
to turn some of the peaceful pastures and enchanting
woodlands into horrific condominiums. But thus far the
stubborn Hamiltonians had managed to keep this little
pocket of the world just the way they liked it.

Dewey's ride in the cool morning air had loosened the
nightmare's grip on her mind; and the sight of George's
house, shining in the early morning sun, restored her to
common sense and to peace with herself. Refreshed, she
turned Starbuck around and headed for home. This was
Hamilton Homecoming day: There was a great deal to be
done. It was going to be a very big day for the little town.

"I think that must be her now!" said a young woman
excitedly to her neighbor. "Yes! Here she comes!"

Howard Street was lined with spectators, all standing
eagerly in the bright morning sunshine, awaiting a glimpse
of Jenny Riley and Alejandro Ponseca as they walked from
the Hamilton Inn to the river. There had been a similar
crowd at the airport yesterday afternoon when Jenny Riley
and her partner were met by Jenny's father, Jack, and a
small delegation of the town's prominent citizens: Fielding
Booker, captain of the tiny Hamilton police force; and
Henrietta Ambler, a horse breeder and the richest person in
town.

Susan Miles glanced at her watch. "The River Festival
starts in ten minutes," she said to Dewey. "I think we'd
better get down to the landing for the big launching."

"Yes, I suppose you're right. There will be plenty of time
to see Miss Jenny Riley." Dewey fixed a big straw hat
firmly down on her head, adjusted her sunglasses, and

picked up an enormous canvas carryall. Susan turned to her husband, Nick, who stood with an air of anticipation, holding a small girl firmly with each hand. "Are you three coming with us?"

Nick Miles, a hearty and cheerful man with an outdoorsman's air, smiled crookedly at Susan, then bent down and whispered to his daughters. They chattered back to him excitedly in stage whispers, and he shook his head at his wife. "You ladies run along," he answered happily. "Meg and Elizabeth want to see the star."

"They do, do they?" asked Susan in a teasing voice as she kissed the girls good-bye. "Bye, Mamma," said Elizabeth, the older one, politely. Meg merely waved abstractedly. "Pick me up, Daddy," she demanded. "I can't see through all these people." Dewey and Susan headed away as Nick Miles hoisted Meg up onto his shoulders.

"Honestly," said Susan, laughing, as she and Dewey made their way down Howard Street toward the river, "the men in this town have gone ga-ga!"

"Don't I know it," agreed Dewey. "George is holding out a forlorn hope that Jenny Riley will teach him to tango."

Susan giggled. "I suppose all things are possible," she answered.

"In this best of all possible worlds," finished Dewey.

It was a bright sunny day, without a hint of clouds in the sky. Already the town had a festive air: families stood in clusters of anticipation along Howard Street, or made their way in small cheery packs to Adams Landing. As Dewey and Susan made their way to the river, the aroma of hot dogs and baking potatoes wafted up to greet them. Dewey had all but forgotten her nightmare, until Susan brought up the subject of Professor Renfrew's lecture.

"That man positively terrified me last night," she confided. "I told Nick about it, but, of course, he thinks I'm crazy anyway, so I shouldn't have looked to him for comfort."

Dewey nodded. "There was something frightening about that whole thing," she agreed. "I don't know what he can think of us, to come home to Hamilton and scare the living daylights out of us all like that. Nick was unsympathetic?"

"Worse than that. He kept pretending to hear noises outside. Thank heavens the girls were asleep!"

"Sometimes husbands just don't fill the bill," said Dewey. "At least I had Isaiah with me last night. He has never in his long and virtuous life laughed at my fears."

"A wonderful dog," agreed Susan with feeling. She and Nick were the unhappy owners of a half-crazed mutt who detested strangers and family alike. He spent his days and nights in gloomy solitude in a small run near the back porch, growling his menace. "I would hate to have to depend on General Barker for help. He would just sit by and watch as the high priests came to get us for the sacrifice."

Dewey nodded. "It's time you found a new home for that dog, Susan."

"I'd love to—but they don't have homes for delinquent dogs. Besides, what he needs is reform school."

"Maybe a job. He'd make a good watchdog for the cemetery, you know. And old Gottlieb—Bill Bentley's dog—is on his last legs."

"Don't talk about cemeteries!" said Susan with a shiver.

The river bank at Adams Landing sloped gently down. Here the river was wide and the current flowed in a strong but even and predictable course; on this bank there was a small marina, in a protected cove, where a few Hamiltonians kept their waterlogged old tubs. There were one or two smarter craft among the assortment: Morgan Stern, a retired boxer with a penchant for reciting the poetry of A. E. Housman, lived in a neatly kept houseboat called the *Halfpenny*, which was tied up at the far end of the marina. And of course, Henrietta Ambler had rather a nice little cabin cruiser, the *Leg Up*, which she took out from time to time when she was entertaining her racing friends. But most of the traffic on the river was of the light commercial sort; the fishing was not what it once had been, and the waters were only beginning to make a comeback from the dark days of heavy pollution.

A fair crowd had started to gather near the large yellow and white marquee.

"Look, Dewey." Susan nudged her friend. "There's Alfred Scott. Is it true he put you in his novel?"

"Good gracious, no!" replied Dewey, blushing. "He says he has a librarian as a character, but from what I gather, she's twice the woman I ever dreamed of being at her age."

"Or half the woman." Susan giggled. "At least, if his book is a big success, maybe Abby will be able to stop working for a while."

"You know, I think Abby took that job at the nursery because she wanted to," mused Dewey. "They haven't ever been hard up—even if Henrietta Ambler does keep Abby on a tight leash. Alfred inherited *some* property from his father, and he sold it for a fortune."

"Either she wants to—or she needs to get away from Alfred."

"I imagine Abby likes to work."

"Some do and some don't," agreed Susan. She was rather sensitive on this point, as Dewey knew. Susan had given up her law practice after the birth of her second daughter, Meg; and although she talked, from time to time, of going back to it, Dewey had long sensed that Susan's heart was far from the dull and dusty documents of her profession.

"Anyway, I do think they're hard up," Susan went on.

"You're not serious? Abby Scott's mother is the richest woman in Hamilton!"

"Well—now, don't quote me on this—but I heard from Todd Fenton—Sergeant Fenton's cousin, you know, at the garage—that Alfred was trading in the Mercedes."

"But that doesn't mean anything. Maybe he got tired of it. Wanted something more unusual."

"For a Ford," said Susan firmly.

"Oh!" Alfred Scott had never been known to drive an American-made car in his life. This certainly was news. "My goodness! I hope he hasn't been gambling again. Henrietta will have a fit. And I doubt Alfred likes the idea of asking his mother-in-law for a loan."

"No," agreed Susan. "The advance from Harbison House will come in pretty handy, I'd bet."

Dewey watched the tall figure of Alfred Scott, who was helping with the sound system; he was twisting a spindly microphone in its stand. Next to him, looking smartly aware, accessible, and sympathetic, was Gerald Davidson, a junior United States senator whose first term was coming to a close. He glanced casually at a fistful of index cards. "Good heavens!" thought Dewey as she and Susan settled themselves in folding metal chairs. "Can't he even launch a rowboat without calling on his speech writer?" Dewey had little use for politicians of the slick modern school. She preferred the plain-spoken scoundrels of the old days.

Davidson's wife, Nancy, was not a Hamilton native, although she had been at pains, over the last six years, to establish a condescending rapport with the townspeople. Naturally, most people in town despised her for it. Today Nancy Davidson was dressed to the nines; she smiled vaguely at the crowd and adjusted the white ribbon at the neck of the champagne bottle that would christen Sid Smith's rowboat, the *Trollin' Along*.

Smith, appearing well scrubbed and uncustomarily sober for such a late hour on a Saturday morning, shifted self-consciously from foot to foot and squinted into the crowd. He was unused to the daylight.

On the boat landing the Hamilton Volunteer Fire Department, suited up in their smartest denim, were at the ready. These burly men and strong women, five in number, would send the *Trollin' Along* down the padded sides of the trailer and into the river as soon as Nancy Davidson had done her bit and cracked the bottle over the bow.

George Farnham stepped up to the little podium and made a few introductory remarks, thanking people for their support and pointing out, in the crowd, the dozen or so far-flung Hamiltonians who had returned home for this festive alumni weekend. Each of the visitors stood to be acknowledged as his or her name was called out, amid a thin spattering of inattentive applause.

Suddenly the little crowd in the tent was galvanized to action. This was the moment they had been waiting for. Everyone stood as Jenny Riley—tall, lissome, and still the sleepy-eyed beauty that the town remembered—made her way slowly toward the rank of chairs at the front reserved for the honored guests of the day. Walking at her side was a tall, lean man with dark features, flashing eyes, and perfect grace. "Look—here she comes!" said Susan with a smile. "Dewey, I think Alejandro Ponseca is positively dreamy. Don't you?"

"Yes, indeed," said Dewey appreciatively.

Alejandro Ponseca was a decidedly handsome man. He walked with the grace of a cheetah, in long, sure, liquid strides, with his head erect and shoulders back. He looked utterly at his ease; and Dewey watched in amusement as his eyes scanned the crowd, stopping briefly here and there to take in the glance of a woman. There could be no question about it, she thought as his eyes met hers with a piercing, intimate regard. Alejandro Ponseca was an old-fashioned lady-killer.

"I think," said Susan Miles softly, "that his dancing tonight is sure to be a crowd-pleaser."

"Without a doubt," replied Dewey abstractedly. Her attention had been caught by someone on the other side of the crowd. It was Mildred Jones, mother of Tommy. Dewey thought she had never in her life seen such concentrated hatred in a person's face. "Without a doubt," she repeated.

7

"As you know, the winning hat in tonight's Straw Hat Contest has been selected for its artistry, inventiveness, and practicality, as determined solely by me," said George Farnham, bestowing a deprecating smile on the assembled guests at the Straw Hat Supper. "After much lengthy and democratic internal debate, I have at last decided upon the Chosen Hat."

"George Farnham has missed his calling," remarked Henrietta Ambler to Dewey James. "He's an autocrat manqué."

"What's manqué about it, Henrietta?" responded Dewey. "George rules the roost with an iron will. You just don't see him in operation. Leithdown Farm doesn't pay much attention to the little doings of the town council meetings."

On the small plywood stage in the Great Hall of the Grain Merchants' Exchange Building, George Farnham paused dramatically, waiting for the anticipation to gather. Before him, clustered around several dozen large tables, were the two hundred and fifty Hamiltonians who had turned out for the evening's festivities. George Farnham had spent the entire dinner hour cruising up and down through the crowd, stopping to admire hats and, in a few instances, to try them on. He had finally made his selection.

"Come on, George!" shouted someone from the crowd.

"The suspense is killing us!" clamored another voice.

Farnham whisked a small piece of paper from his jacket pocket and donned his spectacles. "Ahem." He looked out at the assembled diners, all in a cheerful postprandial state. "The winner of a dinner for two at Panella's Italian Villa is . . . Barry Duke!" said George, in his best emcee's voice.

There was thunderous applause in the cavernous room, and cheers echoed loudly off the granite walls. Wearing his prizewinning hat—which looked like something out of Fritz Lang's *Metropolis*—Barry Duke, Hamilton's leading and only dealer in rare books, rose to claim his prize. In the corner the band chimed in with the opening strains of "Pomp and Circumstance" as Duke made his way to the makeshift plywood stage. On his head was a huge sombrero, made of computer diskettes that had been put together shingle-style, with large diskettes for the brim and the smaller size for the crown. Barry Duke smiled, doffed his ridiculous hat, and bowed to the cheering audience.

"That was *very* clever," said Henrietta Ambler in her deep voice. "Computer things. What do they call those things, Dewey?"

"Diskettes, Mrs. Ambler," put in Tom Campbell hastily. Campbell never missed an opportunity to curry favor with the few people in Hamilton whom he considered his social equals. "Professor Renfrew was just remarking on how up-to-date we are in Hamilton. Having a sense of humor about computers, he feels, shows that we are a truly progressive community."

"Hmmm," said Henrietta Ambler, adjusting a diamond bracelet on her wrist and looking at Campbell suspiciously. She was a regal redhead of indeterminate age and infinite fortune. A widow for many years, she was much sought after by a variety of men, but she suspected them all (and rightly) of merely being after her money. There certainly wasn't much else to love about Henrietta Ambler. "Is Professor Renfrew the thoroughly modern man who discussed ritual sacrifice last night at the library?" she asked archly.

"Yes, indeed," replied Campbell. "You see, the professor's thesis holds that—"

"Quite a clever idea."

"What—ritual sacrifice, Henrietta?" asked Dewey.

"Well—yes, of course, that too. Providing you choose

your victim well." She looked straight at Tom Campbell as she said this. "But I *was* referring to Barry Duke's hat. You can just put your files on your head, whenever you have to go anywhere, and then whisk them out when you get where you're going. I like it. I imagine you could save a great deal in photocopying fees that way."

Dewey laughed. Like most very wealthy people, Henrietta Ambler was a notorious skinflint. "The hat is rather clever. I wonder how he got all those little things to keep from sliding out of their envelopes?"

"It's just the kind of thing you ought to put in your next spy book, Alfred," continued Henrietta Ambler, ignoring Dewey and turning a basilisk eye on her son-in-law. Alfred Scott tried to look suitably impressed with the idea.

"Marvelous suggestion, Henrietta, marvelous." He regarded her nervously. "Hah! Maybe it's not too late to make a change in my present book."

"Oh, Lord, Alfred, any KGB agent worth his salt would spot it in a minute," retorted his mother-in-law. "What on earth is the matter with you tonight? I've never seen you so jumpy. For that matter, what is the matter with everyone? And Alfred—*where* is Abby?"

"Oh—nothing at all wrong with me. But Abby—she's—well, she didn't feel up to the party this evening."

"Speak *up*, Alfred. Don't mumble. What on earth has gotten into you? I've never known *you* to play the sycophant. Have you run out of money or something? Don't tell me you've been laying off bets again, Alfred. You won't get a nickel from me, you know."

"Dessert, anyone?" Susan Miles interjected brightly.

"Susan, we've already had dessert," said Nick, who received an abrupt kick on the shin from Dewey. Nick was quite right: They had had dessert—tiny little fruit tarts, all lovingly made by hand by George Farnham, the acknowledged Escoffier of Hamilton. But everyone—everyone but Nick, that is—knew what Susan meant.

"I wonder if we could get seconds," said Dewey in soothing tones. "Alfred?"

Alfred Scott leaped up to go in search of more tarts, and the band started to tune their instruments.

"God, that man is useless!" complained Henrietta Ambler as she watched her son-in-law search for more tarts.

Nils Reichart took over the microphone from George.

"Ladies and gentlemen," he said, "I'd like to get the Dance Competition underway." He issued some instructions for clearing the floor, leaving a large empty space before the stage. The observers took up positions around the great room or headed straight for the bar, according to their predelictions. Finally everything was at the ready.

George Farnham rushed over to Dewey's table and scooped her up. "Pardon us, everyone. Stand back. You are about to witness the most amazing dance partnership since Vernon and Irene Castle."

"George, aren't your forgetting Fred and Adele?" asked Tom Campbell.

"Oh, Tom, do shut up," said Henrietta Ambler. "Go on, you two. We'll all be pulling for you." She turned on Tom Campbell. "Who brought you up, young man?" She gave him a withering look and left the table.

Dewey and George made their way to the dance floor. The contest had simple rules: Couples were to be judged on their consistency, stamina, and enjoyment. Fancy footwork was fine, if you were prepared to keep it up all night; but it wouldn't do to take a few wild steps in order to impress the judge. Nils Reichart would be looking chiefly at the whole effect. And at any rate he was predisposed to favor amateurs.

"I know all of our contestants tonight want to shine," said Reichart, "especially because we are honored to have two of the world's finest dancers here in the audience tonight." He nodded toward the VIP table near the front of the room, where Jenny Riley sat with her partner. Next to her, looking proud and just a little bit moonstruck, was Fielding Booker, captain of the Hamilton Police. Jack Riley sat across the table from his daughter, scowling at Nancy Davidson, the senator's wife; the senator himself, never one to miss a campaign opportunity, was glad-handing his way through the room in an obvious manner.

Alejandro Ponseca was on Jenny's left. Dewey watched as, with a single smile, he corralled the attention of Henrietta Ambler. He rose and held out a chair for her; she looked him up and down with interest and then accepted his offer. Dewey watched her with amusement. Henrietta Ambler smiled and laughed as Ponseca leaned in close to her; even from this distance Dewey could see that the icy Henrietta accepted his compliments as if he spoke the truth. Dewey was impressed. It had been a very long time since she had seen Henrietta Ambler laugh.

Leaning up against a far wall, watching the table intently, was Alfred Scott. He didn't look happy; but then, perhaps he missed having Abby here with him, Dewey reflected. Or perhaps he quite reasonably detested his mother-in-law.

"I believe all systems are go," said Nils Reichart over the tuning noises of the band. "So—let's start with a proverb. It's one I learned on a trip to Louisiana. *Mes chers, laissez les bon temps rouler*—let the good times roll!"

Thirty couples took to the floor. There were to be six dances: two fox trots, a waltz, a polka (which was also the elimination dance), and a cha-cha; the last dance was freestyle.

By the end of the second fox trot the field had narrowed considerably. Two of the younger couples, dismayed by the music, perhaps, had left the floor almost immediately. A handful of others, deciding that they were distinctly out-classed, had sat down to watch. That left twenty-two competing couples on the dance floor.

It was time for the waltz. Dewey watched in dismay as Norman Fox and Delphine Charlotte whirled in great and small circles about the floor, never missing a beat. "Oh, George!" she said sadly. "We haven't got a chance." She nodded toward the dance instructors.

"Now, now, my dear. This is no ordinary contest. I think we may have more to fear from that young couple over there." He turned, and Dewey turned with him. Over his shoulder she could see young Amy Freeman with her boyfriend. "They have style."

"You're so right," Dewey agreed. She looked again at Norman and Delphine. "You know, they're letter-perfect, those two, but I'd swear she can't stand to touch him."

"You're projecting."

"Oh, heavens, George, I am not. Look at them." And as they made their next turn, George took a good look.

"Hmm. Seem to be having some sort of argument. Wouldn't you say?"

Dewey nodded vigorously. "I would, indeed. I wonder why they choose to fight their fight here. It would be so much simpler to duel in the morning, at work."

"Maybe they're—you know—in love or something."

"Good heavens, George, that is really reaching. Even for an incurable romantic like you."

George looked at Dewey tenderly. "There's only one medicine for me, my sweet," he said gently as the music came to an end.

"Well done, contestants!" called Nils Reichart from the stage, saving Dewey the necessity of a reply. "The next dance is our elimination dance. I'll tap the shoulders of couples who are eliminated; they are asked to move from the dance floor right away so that the judging may continue unobstructed. Ready?"

The bandleader nodded, and the group struck up the beginning notes of "Shall We Dance?" George whisked Dewey off in a lively polka step; they kept it up breathlessly, up and down the huge expanse of the Great Hall, as Nils Reichart made his slow and unforgiving way through the dancers, tapping here, tapping there, and sending disappointed couples off to the bar for refreshments.

When the polka was over, Dewey and George remained on the floor, untapped. "We're in, George!" she said excitedly. "Only the cha-cha and the freestyle to go!" She looked around as she caught her breath. There were but three couples remaining on the floor: Dewey and George; Amy Freeman and her boyfriend, Phil; and Delphine and Norman. "Do you think we really have a shot at it?"

George nodded happily. "In like Flynn, my dear. In like Flynn. You watch: Reichart would never give the prize to professional dancers. Wouldn't be sporting. Surprised they were even allowed to enter. And the cha-cha will take care of those youngsters."

But in this George was wrong. Amy and Phil cha-chaed well; they had evidently been practicing. Their steps were rather formal and had a rehearsed look, but they turned out and did the chase step with great enthusiasm, if not expertise. As the band thumped out a heavy rhythm, however, there was a surprise in store. Suddenly and without warning, Delphine shot out an arm and slapped Norman Fox across the face. Then she turned on her heel and stormed off the dance floor.

Norman Fox, stunned, reached for his hair. (Aha! thought Dewey. She had rather suspected that his thatch was not altogether real.) He made a slight and embarrassing adjustment to his scalp, then slunk off the field of battle just as the music stopped. Dewey watched him go with interest. His path took him straight by Jenny Riley's table; for an instant it appeared as though he might stop to speak to her. But at the last minute he veered off to the left, avoiding her table neatly, and disappeared into the crowd.

"Maybe he stepped on Delphine's toes," said George.

"One way or another," agreed Dewey. She studied Jenny Riley with interest. Was it possible that those two knew each other?

"Well, now, friends," said Nils Reichart. "We seem to have narrowed the field once again. Just in time, too, for our last dance—a freestyle. Everybody 'in the mood'?" He turned to the band, who took up that ageless Glenn Miller tune with relish.

Despite their enthusiasm and their youth, Amy and Phil were not slated to carry the day. The freestyle was their undoing; in a last-ditch attempt to show off some of the fancy moves they had picked up at the Youth Center, they reached too far; and as Phil gamely tried to flip Amy over his back, the two of them came crashing down in a heap.

Dewey and George finished up the dance with the cheerful self-consciousness of virtuous victors.

There was thunderous applause as Nils Reichart proclaimed them the winners of the First Ever Hamilton Homecoming Dance Competition. Dewey accepted her crown—a tiara of popcorn—and insisted that Amy and Phil be given the Icarus Award. "For dancing too close to the sun," she said cheerily into the microphone.

8

NOW EVERYONE TOOK to the dance floor. It was a quarter to ten: the grand finale—the dance numbers by Jenny and Alejandro—would start at ten-fifteen sharp.

The two stars had departed for a row of small offices on the second floor, which had been turned into dressing rooms for the occasion. Alfred Scott, once more lending his expertise to all things electrical, had rigged the sound system and then gone upstairs to the rear of the gallery to man the spotlight.

Dewey and George made their breathless way to the bar, accepting congratulations as they went. Senator Davidson stepped up to shake their hands. "A very impressive performance, you two!" he thundered. "I could use a few people like you on my campaign trail. Never seen such stamina. You outlasted the new generation. Well done, well done."

"Thank you, Senator," said Dewey politely. She was desperately thirsty, but the senator stood firmly between her and the bar. "And thank you so much for coming to our party. We're awfully proud of our success stories, here in Hamilton." The senator beamed, then darted off as he caught sight of Henrietta Ambler. George gave Dewey a look.

"George, I'm dying of thirst," she pleaded.

"Onward, my dear," George said encouragingly. The crowd surrounding the bar was tightly packed, and the going was slow.

Fielding Booker emerged, carrying a tray with two frosty

52

glasses on its surface. "Well done, Dewey," said Fielding Booker politely, bowing to her. "Well done, George."

"Thank you, Bookie," said Dewey, eyeing the glasses.

"Why, Bookie—are those refreshments for our parched and victorious throats?" Farnham indicated the tray.

"Afraid not. But they won't make you two wait for a drink. No—I'm on an errand of mercy. Been asked to deliver a beverage to Miss Jenny Riley." Booker beamed, failing utterly to hide his delight. "See you two later," he added, hastening off toward the huge marble staircase against the far wall.

"George!" whispered Dewey as they pressed on through the crowd. "I do believe Amor has shot an arrow!"

"Straight into Fielding Booker's heart. My, my," said George with a smile. "Fielding Booker! In love with Jenny Riley! How he has the nerve, the old dog—"

"Your envy is showing, George."

"Bah! He must be twice her age. It's just infatuation." They had reached the bar, at long last. "What will you have, Dewey?"

"Something exotic, I think. Campari with club soda."

George raised a brow. "My, my, how Conteenental we have grown." He spoke to the barman. "Campari with soda for the Queen of the Hop, if you please. And a bourbon and water." George smiled at Dewey. "You're quite a gal, my dear. I thank you for this evening's success. You were wonderful."

"Good gracious, George. All I did was follow your lead." They raised their glasses, clinked, and sipped.

"Ahh!" said George. "Welcome relief. Now let's see if we can possibly find seats for the main event."

Dewey looked around. "There's Susan—she's waving to us. Come on, Gunga Din."

They made their way back through the crowd. In the stone-walled room, the noise was deafening. The band played on, but by now people had begun to pull their metal folding chairs out onto the dance floor, determined to get a good seat for the show. Just as Dewey and George settled into their seats, the lights in the Great Hall went down. Up on the second-floor gallery a few spotlights sprang up, and to thunderous applause from Hamiltonians of every stripe, Jenny Riley and Alejandro Ponseca leaped upon the plywood stage and began their legendary and provocative "Tango Desperado."

Their dancing was sensual and liquid, but the raised stage allowed the audience a full appreciation of the amazing footwork involved in the "Tango Desperado." Jenny's lean, muscular body was tightly swathed in a glittering gold lamé dress that swooped and twirled as she moved across the floor. Ponseca, looking astonishingly handsome in white tie, moved with her faultlessly. Susan Miles smirked as her husband leaned forward, watching Jenny's every move with an intensity that he usually reserved for *Monday Night Football*.

"Just look at Nick," she whispered to Dewey. Dewey nodded and cocked her head to indicate George Farnham, who was similarly captivated. Dewey looked around. Every member of the audience was deeply caught up in the tantalizing performance. From her seat Dewey could just make out the milky shine of Professor Renfrew's glasses; he was nodding his head in tempo, watching intently. Even Henrietta Ambler, who had commandeered a chair next to Senator Davidson, looked pleased. Dewey thought it was too bad that Norman Fox and Delphine Charlotte had missed out on this. How strange their departure had been! She wondered briefly again at Norman Fox's behavior. He was a thoroughly unlikable man, she thought.

The dancing went on. How they could keep it up! Dewey was filled with admiration as she took in the highly developed muscles of Jenny Riley's back and legs. This South American tango was really much more physically demanding than she had imagined—and there was nothing about it that smacked of the slow, slightly sleazy "tango" that was caricatured and parodied on dance floors all across the world. These dances were intricate, highly stylized, and playful adventures in rhythm and grace. Enormously complicated, thought Dewey, and absolutely mesmerizing.

Jenny and Alejandro danced for a full twenty-five minutes. When the music finally stopped after the last song, the performers, smiling broadly, took proud bows and hastened off the stage as the audience, on its feet, clamored for more. Dewey watched as the couple headed up the ancient marble staircase toward their makeshift dressing rooms.

George Farnham rose and went to the microphone to announce that the Homecoming Festival had raised nearly four thousand dollars for the library's Computer Fund. A cheer went up, and Tom Campbell and Dewey were called on to speak to their assembled neighbors. Dewey made it brief; the hour was late, and everyone (including herself) wanted to go home. But Tom Campbell, once started on his perorations, showed no signs of stopping.

"And in conclusion," Campbell was saying, "I should like to thank Professor Renfrew—"

"Thank you very much, Tom," said George Farnham firmly, taking the microphone from the zealous librarian. "And once again, our thanks to you all for making—"

Suddenly there was a cry from the second floor. Alejandro Ponseca, half-dressed, his hair flying wildly, charged out of one of the small rooms that opened onto the gallery. "Help!" he cried desperately, leaning over the gallery railing. "A doctor! Help!"

An unhappy murmur went up from the crowd. Fielding Booker raced up the stairs toward the gallery; Lisa Nelson, a young GP, made her way briskly through the crowd and followed him. People began a rush toward the staircase; Nils Reichart stood and grabbed for the microphone, making a plea for order. George Farnham took up a post at the bottom of the stairs, firmly refusing to let anyone but the doctor and the police force go past. Sonny Royce, who had been covering the party for the Hamilton *Quill*, got a picture of the distraught Alejandro Ponseca as he leaned out over the balcony, pleading for help.

Henrietta Ambler rose and looked panic-stricken at Ponseca. He put his head down heavily on his arms as Booker and Dr. Nelson rushed past behind him. The crowd below could see them entering the small office along the gallery hallway.

"Alejandro!" called Henrietta Ambler, but she could not make herself heard above the increasing noise of the crowd. "Alejandro! Alejandro!" she called out wildly.

Directly above her, leaning heavily on the gallery rail, Ponseca was sobbing loudly. "My Jenny!" he cried. "My darling Jenny! Don't leave me!"

9

FIELDING BOOKER SHOOK his head grimly. Jenny Riley lay on the floor in the makeshift dressing room, in utter and alien repose. Her body still glistened with perspiration from the exertions of her glorious performance. But she was most decidedly dead.

Next to her outstretched hand was a glass, its contents spreading in a slow stream across the wooden floor.

Lisa Nelson rose from her examination and looked at Booker, her face impassive. "My guess is that she has been poisoned, Captain."

Booker's handsome features were shot through with pain. He looked at the glass on the floor and then at Dr. Nelson. There was a question in his eyes. Dr. Nelson answered it. "We'll have to wait for the postmortem, but at a guess— yes. She must have taken a drink after her dance. It seems the likely means."

"Very well. Thank you, Doctor. Will you please telephone to the county medical examiner and ask them to send someone right away?" Dr. Nelson nodded. "And send my sergeant, Mike Fenton, if you can find him, please. Thank you. And—Doctor—please tell George Farnham that no one is to leave the premises without my say-so. We'll need the names and addresses of all of the guests, as well as the catering staff. Thank you."

Dr. Nelson departed, and Fielding Booker sat down heavily on a chair. He remained immobile for several moments until he was disturbed from his reverie by Alejandro Ponseca.

"If you please, Officer, I should like to say good-bye."

Ponseca stood in the doorway, his muscular body looking awkward and shadowy in the dim light.

At once Booker was all business. "I'm sorry, sir. No one is to enter this room." He rose and ushered Ponseca out into the hallway, looking at him darkly. "You had better get your clothes on immediately. We will have to ask you some questions."

Ponseca nodded like one in a trance and made his way softly back down the hall to another office, which was his changing room. Booker watched him go with a heavy heart. Then he turned and looked once more at the beautiful and unmoving figure of Jenny Riley.

Fielding Booker had been captain of Hamilton's tiny police force for half a dozen years; for two decades before that, he had been second in command, under Dewey James's late husband, Brendan. Booker was a good-looking man of fifty-five or so; powerfully built, with an imposing brow and a knack for sartorial elegance that was charming, if incongruous, in a small-town cop. Dewey James, who knew him well, sensed that Booker had once felt himself destined for great things; he had a potent romantic streak, and she felt that perhaps, in his youth, he had dreamed of one day becoming a great private detective or a special consultant to Scotland Yard. He certainly had the requisite panache.

Unfortunately, Hamilton's stylish and handsome policeman would never be a legendary crime-stopper. He had class, and elegance, but he was fettered in his climb to greatness by a sadly workaday intellect. Dewey loved him dearly anyway, despite his limitations, and she always had; it was she who had given him his nickname "Bookie," when, as a young officer, he had helped to corner some gangsters who were putting the squeeze on local racehorse owners.

In the little office off the gallery Booker shook his head as he looked at the situation before him. Certainly, over the years, he had proved himself competent to handle most of the infringements of the law that cropped up in his peaceable domain. Once or twice, he had to admit, he had been aided by the—the—*intrusion* was too strong a word; the unsolicited advice, perhaps, of some of his fellow citizens. Of *one* fellow citizen in particular. He walked out to the gallery railing and looked down at the crowd in the Great Hall below. He spotted Dewey, who was sitting perfectly still at one of the tables, looking across the room. The Lord only knew what crazy notions might be already racing through that brain of hers. Booker hoped to God that he could solve this case before dotty old Dewey James saw fit to put her nose in it.

At 1:00 A.M. a few stragglers were still milling about in the Great Hall. The ambulance had come and taken Jenny Riley away; and Booker, having made sure of the names and addresses of all of the guests and staff, had at last sent everyone home.

Jack Riley, however, had been unable to leave. Since the news of Jenny's death had reached him, he had not moved from his seat. He sat there still, unmoving, staring dully into space.

George Farnham was beside him, watchful. George knew the power of grief to overwhelm the mind; when his own wife died, he had been wildly unaccepting of her loss for many months. He could not imagine this greater pain, this infinitely more unjust bereavement. He could not imagine the loss of a child.

And so George was content to sit quietly with Jack Riley while the crowd dispersed; while a sobbing Alejandro Ponseca bid good night to Jenny's father; while one by one Jack Riley's friends and neighbors departed, leaving him with his pain.

Across the room Dewey waited patiently. There was nothing she could do to help Jack Riley, but perhaps she could at least give him a lift home.

The county medical team had come and gone. Now the staircase leading to the gallery was sealed off with yellow scene-of-crime tape; a young woman police officer had been stationed at the foot of the stairs and another young officer at the top of the marble flight. Upstairs there had been for a time the occasional flash of light from the police photographer's camera and a steady coming and going of personnel. But now even these activities had ceased. Dewey looked up and saw Fielding Booker donning his old-fashioned homburg. At his side was Sergeant Fenton. The two men looked somber as they descended the stairs and ducked under the yellow tape.

Mike Fenton approached Dewey. "Mrs. James, ma'am, I'm going to have to ask you to leave."

"Yes, of course, Mike. I was only waiting for George." They turned and looked across the room, where Farnham was helping Jack Riley to his feet. "He came with me, you see."

"Yes. Well." Fenton looked to Booker, who shook his head firmly. "We'll see that Mr. Farnham gets home safely."

"Just a minute, Mike," said Farnham, approaching. He looked carefully at Dewey. "You all right, my dear?"

"Yes, George, I'm fine. What on earth happened?"

"We'll talk about that later," he replied firmly. "You and I are going to take Jack home. Then I'll see you home. Will that suit you?"

"Of course." She stood and reached for her bag.

"Meet you out front in five minutes."

Dewey headed out into the night. "Oh, dear me," she said to herself with a sinking feeling in her stomach. "Professor Renfrew seems to have got his blood sacrifice."

10

"I TELL YOU, George, I don't *care* what you think of the man. He is a suspect in a murder investigation. He must not be allowed to have access to the evidence." Senator Gerald Davidson was pacing up and down in George Farnham's kitchen, an unlighted cigar in one hand, a cup of hot coffee in the other.

"Really, Senator, I think you're making a mistake." George Farnham sipped at his own coffee and leaned back comfortably in his chair. "Sit down, Senator, please."

"Sit *down?* A murder is committed, right out in the open, right under the nose of a United States senator, and you have the temerity to ask me to sit down?" He glowered at Farnham, put down his coffee, and leaned heavily on the kitchen table. "You must think this is just some kind of random crime. I don't see it that way. And Henrietta—Mrs. Ambler—has taken a personal interest in the matter. I don't think I have to spell it out for you, George, what that means. That lady gets what she wants in this town. And when she asks me to fulfill a commission for her, by God, I do it. Now. Will you oblige me? Or do I have to go over your head?"

George smelled money. Campaign money. But he let it pass—even politicians had to eat. "Senator, please. Fielding Booker is one of the most respected men in town—in the county, for that matter. I think you are doing us all a disservice—Mrs. Ambler, most particularly—if you allow this fantasy to get out of hand. Fielding Booker no more murdered that girl than you did, Senator."

"Oho! So now I'm a suspect, too, is that right?"

"You know perfectly well what I meant. Please, *Gerald*, sit down. You're making me antsy."

Gerald Davidson sat. But he was still angry. "Do you know what they'll make of this town in the press if they get wind of a police cover-up?"

"Who's 'they'? Don't be absurd. Nobody in his right mind has the slightest interest in this little town. And there will be no cover-up."

"You're damn right. I will personally see to it that there isn't. But if you don't cooperate with me on this, George, I will make absolutely certain that you are never elected town council president again. You can kiss your handy little taxpayer-funded office good-bye. *And* your nice fat salary."

George chuckled. "I pay the rent on that little office myself, Senator. A hundred and sixty-two dollars a month. Have to—I still practice law from time to time. And the council job doesn't come with a salary. I do it for free." Gerald Davidson looked disbelieving, but George ignored him. "Listen, Gerald. Hear me out. I am willing to stake my life that Fielding Booker did not murder Miss Jenny Riley. But, if you like, I will keep a weather eye on Fielding Booker's investigation. Will that suit you?"

Gerald Davidson began to be mollified. "I think Mrs. Ambler will find that a satisfactory arrangement. But if I get one whiff—just one whiff—of any funny business, I will personally see that the FBI and the United States Attorney are called in immediately."

"Fine, fine," said Farnham, who knew very well how the FBI and the United States Attorney would laugh at such a suggestion. There wasn't a hint of interstate commerce to this affair; it was purely local. But if the delusion that he walked the corridors of power would get Gerald Davidson out of his hair, George Farnham would let him remain deluded.

"Well, then." Davidson rose. "I'll be on my way." George showed him to the door and then returned to his Sunday breakfast—a powder doughnut from the local carryout, languishing forlornly in a paper bag.

* * *

"What on earth are you talking about, George?" asked Dewey. She and George were seated at her kitchen table, drinking coffee. George had declined her offer of lunch; even in the interests of justice, he was willing to go only so far. He knew the kind of thing Dewey might spring on him, if she chose to be adventurous in the kitchen.

"Apparently, there is no question that Jenny Riley was poisoned last night—that's the preliminary word from the lab. Somehow, Gerald Davidson and Henrietta Ambler have got it into their heads that Bookie ought to be considered a suspect in the murder," replied George. He reached down and scratched Isaiah behind the ear. "Good boy, Isaiah," he told the dog.

"Oh, good heavens. What an idea!" Dewey sat back in her chair, looking thoughtful.

"Yes, I know, my dear. But there isn't a thing I could say to talk him out of it. Henrietta Ambler's got a bee in her bonnet."

"And what a bonnet it is," murmured Dewey.

"Exactly."

"But what gave them that idea in the first place?"

"Dewey—do you remember how, after the dance contest, we met Bookie?"

"Yes—and he was on his way to—oh, good heavens, George! It was the drink that was poisoned? The one Bookie took upstairs?"

"The medical examiner's office isn't finished with their tests yet, but it appears so. And Bookie did take her that drink."

"So he did. My word." Dewey rose and went to fetch the big old-fashioned percolator. She filled their cups, shaking her head. "Poor Bookie! Oh, George, this breaks my heart. Do you remember the look on his face last night?" She looked up sadly from her coffee. "He was like a young man in love."

"He was, wasn't he?" concurred George.

"It's so sad. George—do you know the *Sonnets from the Portuguese*?"

George shook his head.

"There's a lovely bit that Tommy Jones memorized and recited to me one day:

> "The face of all the world is changed, I think,
>   Since first I heard the footsteps of thy soul
>   Move still, oh, still beside me, as they stole
>   Betwixt me and the dreadful outer brink
>   Of obvious death. . . ."

Dewey looked sadly down at Isaiah. "Have you spoken to Bookie?"

George stirred his coffee methodically. "Not yet. And I hope that all of this will blow over—you know how mercurial Henrietta Ambler is. Changes her mind at the drop of a hat. Well." He took a long sip of coffee.

"Is there anything we can do to help?"

George smiled conspiratorially. "The long and the short of it is, my dear, that I have been asked by Henrietta Ambler and Senator Davidson to keep an eye on Booker's investigation."

"They really don't trust him, do they?"

George shrugged. "He took her the drink. Until the M.E.'s office can confirm the medium through which the poison was administered—if it *was* poison, but I think Lisa Nelson was right about that—well, perhaps it's for the best. And they have no quarrel with Mike Fenton. I'm sure that he'll get the ball rolling, even if Bookie does get wind of this nonsense. A good man, Mike."

"Yes—yes, of course he is, George. But if Henrietta Ambler suspects Bookie, won't she be just as ready to think that Mike is in collusion with him?"

"Yes. Ordinarily she might. In fact, that's one of the subjects we touched on this morning, Davidson and I, when he came to call. I gave my word that I'd be on the lookout for any hint of a cover-up."

"Good. That should fix their wagon."

"That's right. Now, my dear, this is where you come in. I'd like to ask you to help me with this business."

"Oh, George. I couldn't possibly. You know how Bookie hates my—my—"

"Meddling?" George smiled broadly. "Your tiresome interference? Certainly, I know that Bookie objects when he feels you are stepping on his toes. But even Bookie would have to admit that you've been helpful to him in one or two little matters over the years."

"Yes, but George—really. Fools rush in."

"And all that. Yes. You're nobody's fool, my dear. But, if you should happen to come across any interesting little fact, you'll let me know, won't you?"

"But, George—this is a delicate situation. I have to be careful not to hurt Bookie's feelings. His and Mike Fenton's."

"If we play our cards right, they won't even get a whiff of this. It will be our little secret, Dewey. Just be yourself. You always get to the bottom of everything, even when you're not trying. So—there you are. Just be yourself."

Dewey grew thoughtful and was silent for a long moment. At last she spoke. "All right, George. I'll help. Because, as a matter of fact, there were one or two things about the events last night that struck me as not ringing quite true."

"Good, good." George rose. "Where will you start, my dear?"

Dewey smiled. "I'll start, I think, at the top. Isn't that what they teach in the business world?" She stood up and gathered about her a large purple cardigan sweater. "I'm going to call on Her Majesty, Henrietta Ambler, to see if I can make her come to her senses."

11

LEITHDOWN FARM, WHICH was just two or three miles out Hillside Road from Dewey's place, was one of the great Hamilton success stories. Henrietta Ambler's husband, Kent, had bought the place more than twenty-five years ago, when he was still a very young man. He had been good with horses, and (with one sad exception) good with people, with a perfect nose for the unrealized potential in a Thoroughbred; as a result, his stud farm had prospered mightily, and in racing circles he was a legend.

His admirers and detractors alike had to admit that Kent Ambler had been smart about horses. He had gone to claiming races with a firmly fixed limit in his mind; and if he had ever exceeded that limit in the purchase of any horse, it was a secret that he had taken with him to the grave. In life, he had likened himself to Michelangelo (modesty was not one of Kent Ambler's virtues); he had been fond of saying that he could see the latent winner in a horse and that he went after it, carving a winner out of a chunk of horseflesh in much the same way that the great Italian had seen masterpieces waiting within the raw marble.

Unfortunately, Kent Ambler's X-ray vision had failed him in the matter of choosing a wife. Henrietta Ambler was shrewd and demanding; her affection was easily won, and just as easily lost; and in the course of her life she had not made many friends in Hamilton. Perhaps it was this great failing that had driven Kent Ambler to an early, drink-induced death. Nobody in town had found fault with his escape route.

Henrietta Ambler had kept the farm in operation after her husband's death. There had been a succession of farm managers; one had lasted almost six months, but the others had departed in a blur. For this reason, she was sometimes referred to as "Mrs. Legree" by the population.

In an effort to occupy her time Henrietta Ambler had taken up the arcane sport of four-in-hand carriage racing, an obsolescent pastime that required vast sums of money and a huge staff. For this reason she was sometimes referred to as "Mrs. Ben Hur" by the population. She spent six or seven months of the year charging all around the world, sending her carriage and horses on special airplanes to competitions with other, like-minded sporting women. Dewey thought it a strange sport, but she was an open-minded woman, disinclined to judge a person's passions.

Fifteen years ago Henrietta and Kent's only child, Abby, had married Alfred Scott, a suitable young man, but rather wet, with enough of his own money to escape the label of gold digger. The marriage, Dewey supposed, had been happy as it could be. She couldn't imagine a worse burden for a young man than having Henrietta Ambler for a mother-in-law.

As she drove up the long, winding road that led to the house, Dewey wasn't worried about an excuse for calling. Henrietta Ambler had made a most generous contribution to the Library Fund, over and above the cost of a ticket to the Straw Hat Supper Dance; it was only natural for Dewey to thank her in person. If, during the course of her visit, Dewey could persuade Henrietta Ambler of Bookie's innocence, well and good. It wouldn't hurt to try, anyway.

Dewey was certain that Henrietta Ambler would be disposed to talk about the events of last night. If Gerald Davidson had called on George at nine o'clock this morning, he must have been summoned to Leithdown at sunrise. Indeed, thought Dewey, Henrietta Ambler had one remarkable bee in that bonnet of hers.

Dewey had always thought the Ambler house was dreadful. On the outside, it was an exact replica of Mount Vernon, down to the last detail of the gardens; and as imitations go, it was undoubtedly of the highest order. But Dewey found it cold and sad. It would be so much more gratifying to invent something new. The only house Dewey would ever want to imitate was Monticello—and to duplicate Mr. Jefferson's methods as well—to reinvent it, over and over again, until she died. But to copy Mount Vernon? Why not the White House?

Dewey knocked at the front door and was admitted by a fearsome manservant called Brant, who stood impassively on the doorsill, neither inviting nor rejecting.

"Good morning, Brant. I'm Mrs. James."

"Yes, madam."

"I was hoping for a word with Mrs. Ambler, if she is free."

"Very good, madam. One moment, please." Brant stepped back to allow her to enter the front hall, and disappeared down a long vestibule.

"Good heavens!" thought Dewey. "At least he didn't say that he would 'ascertain' anything." She waited patiently and looked about her idly. The interior design was not an imitation—but that was all one could say for it. She studied a large modern canvas on the wall—a new addition to Henrietta's collection—and found it sadly wanting in taste and character.

There was a soft footfall behind her, and Brant spoke. "Mrs. Ambler will see you in the morning room. This way, please."

Dewey followed the manservant, thinking idly of Ogden Nash: "When called by a Panther, don't anther." They went through to the morning room, a cheerful, glass-enclosed terrace that looked out onto a garden of early-blooming perennials, where Henrietta Ambler was reclining on a chaise longue.

"Dewey!" she exclaimed huskily, extending a heavily jeweled hand. She wore a white caftan with orange trim that fought with her carrot-red hair; on her feet were satin mules. (What else? Thought Dewey to herself.)

"Hello, Henrietta." Dewey took the proffered hand. "I just thought I'd stop in to thank you so much for your contribution. You have made all the difference to our Computer Fund, you know."

"Only too glad to help. And if I thought another check would induce you to eject that tiresome young man from the premises, I'd write one for you here and now."

"Oh, come now, Henrietta—"

"Dewey, sit down. He's a pompous and arrogant fool. We both know it. No use pretending with me, my dear. We have known each other too long."

"Tom Campbell is very good at his job," said Dewey, taking a seat on a reproduction Louis XVI armchair. "And you know, it's not easy to find a good librarian anywhere these days."

"No, I suppose not." Henrietta Ambler was bored with the subject. "What will you have? Iced tea? Or perhaps a cocktail?"

"Oh, nothing, really—"

"Nonsense. Brant! Damn that man. He disappears just when you want him. Oh, there you are," she said to the servant, who had reappeared silently. "Dewey?"

"Iced tea would be lovely."

"Good. Iced tea for Mrs. James and a martini for me. And Brant—" The servant turned.

"Yes, madam?"

"Please don't forget the olive this time."

"Yes, madam." He departed.

"If you think librarians are hard to find, try finding a decent butler in this country. I tell you. There's nothing wrong with being a servant. It's a good job. But they all seem to think it's beneath them. This fellow has just given me notice. I'm ready to slit my wrists, I'm so upset. Just when I thought I'd broken him in nicely, too."

"That must be very distressing," said Dewey.

"They have no sense of what my father used to call 'stick-to-itiveness.'"

"Indeed," said Dewey.

"Well, my dear. You don't want to hear all of my tragedies. What a bore. But now, about this business last night—it was too awful!"

"Yes, it certainly was."

"Thank heavens for Gerald. Gerald Davidson. I had him out here this morning at the crack of dawn and told him exactly what was what." She leaned forward. "Do you *know*, Dewey, that that policeman actually took that girl the poisoned drink? I'd like to know just how far he thought he would get, hiding the evidence and sweeping it all under the carpet, before the truth came out."

Brant arrived and handed round their drinks.

"Thank you, Brant. That will do."

"Yes, madam."

As Henrietta Ambler took a pull at her martini, Dewey jumped into the breach. "Henrietta, really, you can't think that Fielding Booker would do such a thing."

"Oh, can't I? Well, I do. He's not like Brendan was, you know. When your husband was chief of police in this town, we knew where we were. None of this nonsense about the rights of criminals and so forth. That man thinks he's Sherlock Holmes or something, always wearing a hat. Well, I wouldn't have it, and I told Gerald so. And I sent him round to see poor old George Farnham, to let *him* know that we wouldn't sit still for this kind of thing."

"Henrietta—how do you know it was the drink that was poisoned? And how do you know Jenny Riley *was* poisoned? I haven't heard of any results yet from the medical examiner's office."

Henrietta Ambler looked scandalized. "How do I know? For God's *sake*, Dewey, everyone knows. We were all discussing it last night, when they made us wait and wait to see if we were all down on their idiotic list. As if they don't have my address and telephone number! It was all a smoke screen, clearly. Just to throw us off the scent."

"But, Henrietta. Honestly, now. What reason on earth would Fielding Booker have to wish that girl dead? He hardly knew her."

Henrietta fixed Dewey with a long stare. "You were perhaps having too much fun with George last night to notice, Dewey. But that man had fallen for her like a ton of bricks. Honestly! I've never seen anything *like* it. Absurd. At his age?"

Dewey laughed. "Age hasn't a thing to do with it, Henrietta—you know that as well as I do. Besides which, the effect that Jenny Riley had on Fielding Booker was identical to the effect she had on every man in that room last night. You should have seen Nick Miles. George, too. They were all ga-ga. Loopy."

"Yes—but, Dewey—they didn't all take a poisoned drink to her dressing room. What was Booker doing, going to her dressing room, anyway? He ought to have been keeping the peace. Instead, he's running around committing murders and trying to hide all the evidence."

Dewey had to work to keep from laughing. It really was a preposterous suggestion. But then she thought of Jenny Riley, of that electrifying beauty, now stilled, and she grew somber.

"Henrietta, tell me. Did you see anything, anything at all, that leads you to think the poison was in the drink that Fielding Booker brought to the dressing room?"

Henrietta Ambler shook her head. "I just know it, Dewey dear. In here." She gestured toward her heart.

"Excuse me, madam," said Brant, who had stolen quietly in through the door. "There is a gentleman here to see you."

"You wouldn't recognize a gentleman if you fell over one, Brant. So just say there's a man here. Who is it?"

"A Mr. Ponseca."

"Aahh." Henrietta Ambler polished off her martini and looked coyly at Dewey. "Thank you so much for coming, Dewey. You must come round sometime in the summer for a swim, will you? Bring George. We'll play water polo, or whatever they play in swimming pools. Ta-ta." She held out her hand. Dewey, relieved to find a reason to cut the interview short, followed Brant down the vestibule. In the front hall she stopped to speak briefly to Alejandro Ponseca.

"I'm so terribly sorry, Mr. Ponseca," she said. "We haven't even been properly introduced. My name is Dewey James."

The dancer's eyes filled momentarily with tears. "I thank you, Señora James." He smiled at her warmly, detaining her for a moment with his eyes. Then he headed off in the direction that Dewey had come.

Dewey nosed her dusty old station wagon back down the driveway. At the last curve she had to pull over to make room for an oncoming car. The other car slowed, and she looked out to see Alfred Scott at the wheel of a brand-new Ford.

Scott stopped and rolled down his window. "Afternoon, Dewey."

"Hello, Alfred."

"I've been summoned." He nodded toward the house. "Everything in order up there?"

Dewey smiled. "Seems to be. Your mother-in-law has a caller."

"Oh?"

"Yes—Mr. Ponseca."

"Oho! A gentleman caller, you should have said. Well, well, the old vixen!" He waved and drove on.

"Goodness!" said Dewey aloud as she headed for home. Things were looking very lively in Hamilton.

12

ON THE MONDAY following the tragedy the little town of
Hamilton was buzzing with speculation about Jenny Riley's
murder. By noon the word had spread that it *was* murder—
the preliminary report from the coroner indicated that Jenny
Riley had died as a result of ingesting a sizable amount of
nicotine sulfate—a fast-acting poison, easily obtainable,
and very, very lethal, even in tiny amounts. A chill went up
the spine of every Hamiltonian. Poisoned! In her own
hometown!

Jack Riley was forced to postpone his daughter's funeral
arrangements until all the medical evidence had been
gathered. He bore the hiatus well; and he bore well, too, the
unaccustomed attention of his neighbors, who had come in
a steady stream to his small apartment to pay their condo-
lences. People who had ignored Jack Riley for years now
stopped by with fried chicken or cakes or large baskets of
flowers; and if he found this sudden outpouring of affection
galling, after so many years of neglect, he was too kind, or
too stunned, to say so. It was the price of Jenny's fame, he
supposed, that he must submit to these unwelcome atten-
tions.

George Farnham was one among the many who called;
but George had always been Jack's friend and hadn't faded
away, like the rest of them, as Jack Riley's fortunes and
position in town life diminished.

Gerald Davidson, after delivering his ultimatum to
George Farnham, had hightailed it back to Washington with

his well-dressed wife. But some of the other visitors had been planning to spend a few more days in their old hometown; and Jenny Riley's sensational murder did nothing to change their minds.

Alejandro Ponseca had stayed on. He had undergone several hours of intensive questioning by Captain Booker on Sunday; and he had vowed that he would see this thing through to the bitter end. He would make sure that the person who had killed Jenny was brought to justice. Ponseca was well aware, he told the captain, that there was more than one way to skin a cat.

Professor Renfrew stayed, too. He was giving a lecture at the end of the week at nearby Farrand State University, and although he didn't have family left in Hamilton, he was pleased by the welcome Tom Campbell had shown him. The two of them had dined together every night since last Friday; and Campbell, although disinclined to share the professor with less powerful intellects in town, nonetheless wanted everyone to see his academic prize. He had persuaded the professor to make use of the library, where the two of them engaged in long, lengthy displays of questionable erudition for the benefit of anyone who happened by. Campbell was in seventh heaven and hadn't given a thought to poor Jenny Riley. Professor Renfrew, however, rubbed his hands together. In the library, on Monday afternoon, he took advantage of Campbell's lunch hour to revise his famous lecture; it was now updated to include the episode of Jenny Riley's death.

The town was divided on the subject of Alejandro Ponseca. Some people felt there was no question of his guilt. He was a foreigner, with an accent; he was a dancer from New York, an outsider. Others shook their heads and smiled knowingly: There were two sides to every question. If Ponseca wanted to murder Jenny Riley, there must have been a hundred easier ways to do it in New York. He could nudge her in front of a subway train or take her on a late-night walk through Central Park. Or even break her beautiful neck in rehearsal. There seemed little point in murdering her here, in Hamilton, where he stuck out like the proverbial sore thumb.

But by Monday afternoon a different story, drifting into the minds and consciousnesses of people throughout the town, had begun to take hold.

Was it true that Fielding Booker had turned the entire investigation over to Mike Fenton? Someone had it on the best authority. Was it true that Fielding Booker had taken the poisoned drink to Jenny Riley? It must be so, said the wags. He was seen with that drink in his hand! Besides—he had been madly in love with her, and she had sneered at him. Everyone knew that men of his age were liable to strange passions. Men his age did things like that; they were a little bit off their nut. It was common knowledge.

Nowhere in town had the discussion of Jenny's murder been given greater scope than at the Tidal Wave Beauty Salon, citadel of Hamilton fashion. Doris Bock, proprietress of the Tidal Wave and coiffeuse to Hamilton ladies for forty-five years, was a noted purveyor of local information. When she arrived at work on Monday morning, the phone had rung off the hook with people seeking appointments. She had been forced to pick and choose, to squeeze in the best-informed among her clientele. Susan Miles was Doris Bock's three-o'clock.

"Come now, Doris, you don't mean that," Susan Miles was saying over the running water in the sink. "Nobody with any sense would ever suspect Bookie of murder. That's just crazy."

Doris Bock squirted shampoo on Susan Miles's hair and began to lather her up. As she worked, she talked. "*You* say it's crazy, and *I* say it's crazy. But does George Farnham say it's crazy? No. He has taken over the whole investigation, lock, stock, and barrel, leaving poor old Captain Booker to twist in the wind."

"That's exactly what I heard, too," chimed in Mary Barstow, dental hygienist and full-time man-watcher. Mary was not one of Doris Bock's elect; but unfortunately, she had refused to change her appointment. "It's just not fair at all," she called out from under the bonnet of an enormous old-fashioned dryer. "I think maybe I'll stop by to see him later. He probably needs a friend, with the whole town turning their backs on him like this. It's terrible." She looked down at her fingernails. "Have you got time to give me a quick manicure this afternoon, Doris?"

Doris Bock leaned down and whispered to Susan. "So she can get her claws into poor Bookie? Never." She turned to Mary Barstow. "Sorry, honey. No time today."

"Oh," said Mary Barstow, pouting. "I guess some people just can't make time, even for their best customers."

"Don't you fuss at me, Mary Barstow. I've got Mrs. James in fifteen minutes, and then I'm closing up. You know perfectly well that my sister Irene came to town for the Homecoming."

"Oh."

Doris Bock turned off the water and wrapped Susan Miles's head in a towel. "Over here, Susan."

Susan Miles moved to the large old red chair before the mirror and submitted to being combed. "I wonder if George really believes all this hoo-hah about Bookie," Susan continued.

Doris shook her head. "I heard from Sis Keating this morning that Senator Davidson went to talk to him. It must be serious. I just hope they can straighten it out." She tugged vigorously at Susan's unruly blond locks.

"Ouch! Easy, Doris, please. Not without help, they won't."

"They'll get help." Doris twisted around to look at the clock on the wall. Even after forty-five years in a beauty salon, she still found it impossible to tell time in a mirror. "You'll see in exactly one minute."

On cue the big glass door swung open, and Dewey James entered.

"You're absolutely right, Doris," said Susan. It was well known in town that Dewey James had recently provided vital assistance to Booker in solving some rather grisly puzzles. In fact, some Hamiltonians believed that it was Dewey herself, and not Fielding Booker, who had been the brains behind solving the murder at Evergreen Farm. "It's the cavalry to the rescue. Dewey, where's your steed?"

"What's that? Oh, hello, Susan. Mary." Mary Barstow waved kittenishly at Dewey. "Am I on time, Doris?"

"Yes, indeedy, Mrs. James. Be with you in a minute. Take a seat."

Dewey sat.

"So, Mrs. James, is it true or what?" asked Mary Barstow, flipping impatiently through the pages of a fashion magazine.

"Is what true, Mary?"

"That Mike Fenton thinks Captain Booker murdered her."

"Mary!" exclaimed Doris, shaking her head. "Honestly, child. How do you think rumors get started? I'm ashamed of you."

. Dewey smiled. Doris Bock sowed a healthy crop of rumors every year, right here at the Tidal Wave. But there was no point in mentioning that fact. "No, Mary," she said amicably. "Not for a minute does Mike Fenton believe that."

"Phew!" said Mary. "Because they always stick together, cops. I would hate for it to be any different here."

"Mary, I think you must be just about done under there," said Doris firmly. She reached over and flipped off the dryer, unclipped Mary's curls, and sent her on her way.

As soon as Mary Barstow was safely departed, and Susan Miles was settled under the dryer, Doris began to question Dewey closely about Booker's situation. Mindful of Doris's propensity to chatter away, however, Dewey kept her counsel. She could tell by the look on Susan's face that her protests of ignorance were not as convincing as she might have hoped; but that was all right—Dewey could fill Susan in later. The important thing now was to try to find out what Doris had seen at the Straw Hat Supper Dance. Very little escaped the sharp eyes of Doris Bock.

"You were there, Doris," said Dewey. "You know as much about this sad affair as I do. More, perhaps."

Doris Bock nodded. "There was only one murderer I saw go up those stairs—her dancing partner."

"Well, goodness, Doris. The Great Hall was packed with people. I doubt you could have seen everything. There was quite a lot going on."

"That's for sure. Including the sideshow with that horrible little man," Doris said, viciously thrusting a clip into Dewey's scalp.

Dewey squirmed. "Which horrible little man is that, Doris?"

"You know, the one from Doin' Time. The dance teacher."

"Oh, yes." Dewey's interest was aroused. She had forgotten about Norman and Delphine.

"The slapping contest. You and George were dancing, Dewey. Maybe you missed the dramatics—couldn't see through those stars in your eyes, I'll bet."

Dewey ignored this allusion to her supposed romance with George Farnham. There was no power on earth to persuade Doris that she and George were nothing more than old friends. "Well, of course I noticed that they seemed to be having a contretemps," Dewey replied. "George thought it was a lovers' quarrel."

"Hah!" said Doris. "That just shows how little George Farnham really knows about life in this town."

"Well, goodness gracious, Doris, you could hardly expect him to keep up with all of the romances in town."

"That's as may be. But anybody who knows anything about anything around here knows perfectly well that Delphine Charlotte will never get involved with another man. Not since she got her divorce. She's learned her lesson the hard way."

"So I've heard. Still, *le coeur a ses raisons*, and all that. You didn't happen to notice anything else unusual or out of the way, did you, Doris?" The last few words of Dewey's question echoed eerily as Doris adjusted the bonnet of the hair dryer over her head.

"No. Nothing—except that hat of Barry Duke's." Doris turned up the heat on Dewey's dryer, then began to fluff up Susan Miles's hair. Although Doris Bock had not learned to use a blow dryer, the younger generation still came to her. No blow dryer on earth gave satisfaction like half an hour at the Tidal Wave. "Anyway, everyone in town knows that Spaniard did it."

Dewey looked her annoyance. "If you mean Mr. Ponseca, Doris," she called over the noise of the dryer, "you must be aware that nobody knows any such thing. And he's not a Spaniard. I believe he's from Argentina."

"All the same—South Americans." Doris brushed and fluffed at Susan while Dewey dried.

"He was right up there with her on the gallery," Doris Bock went on.

"But why on earth would he do such a thing?" protested Dewey.

"Obvious—it was a crime of passion. You know how they are, those people. He was jealous of Captain Booker. He thought Jenny had been unfaithful to him."

Susan Miles shook her head. "But, Doris, Bookie only met Jenny Riley on Saturday."

"All it takes is an instant, Susan, for a man to fall in love. Everyone knows that. And now poor Captain Booker will be sentenced to death, and that man will go free. There's no justice in this world."

"There's no death penalty in this state," put in Susan mildly with an amused glance at Dewey.

Doris Bock skipped over the point of law and tested Dewey's curls. It never took long under Doris's huge old machine. "What are you going to do about catching him, Dewey? With Captain Booker in jail?" She lifted the bonnet and unpinned Dewey's soft silvery locks.

"Honestly, Doris! Captain Booker isn't in jail at all. He's right behind his desk, where he belongs. And don't you worry about it. He will get his man, I'm sure. He always does," said Dewey modestly.

"I wish I could be sure. Gives me the creeps, a murderer running loose in this town." Doris Bock stepped back and surveyed her handiwork. "You're all finished, Mrs. James. Ready to go out on the town, now. Got any special plans?"

"Nothing special," said Dewey with a wink at Susan Miles. "Just dinner with George."

13

DEWEY STEPPED OUT into the late afternoon sunshine of Howard Street and paused, uncertain what her next step might be. Earlier in the day she had called on George Farnham at his office; he had sketched for her the forensic details that had emerged. The county lab had found traces of nicotine sulfate in the glass found at the scene; Fielding Booker's prints were also on the glass. According to the testimony of Alejandro Ponseca, Jenny had been drinking club soda with bitters—a pale, orange-brown drink. The addition of a very few drops of the poison would have produced a very similar-looking cocktail.

On Saturday night, as the tragedy unfolded, the police had not searched the party-goers for the container that had held the poison; and the catering crew had been well on its way to finishing their cleanup by the time of Jenny's death. Dewey reasoned that the murderer had had a fairly clear field, and an ample amount of time, to hide or discard whatever small vial or jar had been used to bring the poison to the Straw Hall Supper. It was unlikely that the killer would have kept the container on his person after administering the drops.

Sergeant Fenton and Officer Shoemaker, George had told her, had spent the entire day in an inch-by-inch search of the Great Hall. Unlucky Officer Machen had been assigned the singularly aromatic task of searching the garbage. But Dewey did not suppose that, even if they found the container, it would tell them very much.

It seemed to her that one important element of the whole

affair might lie in Jenny's life away from Hamilton—that is to say, her life in New York, her life as the partner of Alejandro Ponseca. She wished she had thought to ask him yesterday, when she had encountered him at Henrietta Ambler's place, how long he planned to stay. But there was an easy way to find out, she supposed. The Hamilton Inn was just a few hundred yards away, on the other side of Howard Street.

"Good afternoon, Mildred," said Dewey to the desk clerk.

"Hi, Mrs. James."

"That was a terrible business the other night, wasn't it?"

"I suppose so," replied Mildred Jones. "It's no secret in this town that I didn't care much for that girl. But I'm sorry she got killed like that." There was a strange light in Mildred Jones's eyes that made Dewey uncomfortable. She wondered if Tommy Jones would ever hear the news of Jenny's death.

"Mildred, I wondered if you could tell me—is Mr. Ponseca still here?"

Mildred Jones looked warily at Dewey. "He is."

"Well, then. Would you mind ringing his room for me, to let him know that I am downstairs, if he could spare me a few minutes?"

"Sure thing." She reached for the telephone and dialed. Dewey took a seat in one of the ancient rose damask wing chairs in the lounge, and waited.

Alejandro Ponseca arrived quickly. His handsome face still looked strained, but even his grief over Jenny's death couldn't subdue the lively grace of the man.

"Mrs. James," he said, looking at her curiously. "The front desk says you wanted to see me?"

"Yes, Mr. Ponseca. If you could spare me a few minutes." She looked over toward the front desk, where Mildred Jones was studying the guest register with careful insouciance. "I wonder if we might go out on the back terrace, where it's more private."

"Why not? It's a lovely afternoon."

They settled themselves in the old-fashioned wicker settees on the back terrace, and Dewey took a deep breath.

"I'm certain you may find me impertinent, Mr. Ponseca, to come calling on you at a time like this."

"Not at all. On the contrary, Mrs. James. I have been told that you have a—certain facility for this kind of affair. In fact, I was on the point of telephoning to you, to ask if you might be willing to help me."

Dewey wondered briefly who Ponseca's source might be. Henrietta Ambler, perhaps. "Good heavens, yes, Mr. Ponseca. If I possibly can."

Ponseca leaned forward and studied Dewey's face intently. "I want to find the person who has done this thing. And bring him to justice. If there could ever be fierce enough justice for such a dog as he."

"How do you know, Mr. Ponseca, that Jenny's killer is a man?"

Ponseca smiled. "I know the kind of feelings she could inspire in a man, Mrs. James. She was a most remarkable woman."

"I see. Well—Mr. Ponseca, I was hoping that you might help me to form a clearer picture of Jenny. No one here in town really knew her."

"So I understand." He shook his head sadly. "She was a flower, Mrs. James. A beautiful flower. I am devastated by her loss."

"Yes, I'm certain you are."

"It seems a great pity that she should perish this way—and not simply because all her life was before her. She was hoping, I think, to find a way into her father's heart once more."

"Yes. It is very sad, the way she and Jack lost touch with each other. You know the story?"

He shrugged. "I know only what she told me, in the few weeks before coming here. Before that time, she never spoke of him."

"And what did she tell you, Mr. Ponseca?"

"That he had—how do you say—discarded her?"

"Disowned her."

"That is the very word that she used." He nodded. "On account of a disagreement they had, when she left home. But she had written to him, to say that she was coming home and wanted to make peace between them. He replied, but I don't know in what manner."

"What did Jenny tell you?"

"She mentioned, on the night before we came here, that she hoped she would not disappoint him."

"Oh, my. How sad." Dewey thought this a clear indication that the old wounds had begun to heal. "Was she looking forward to seeing other friends here in Hamilton, Mr. Ponseca?"

"That I do not know. But—I had a feeling."

"Yes?"

"This will sound to you as though I am being dramatic, Mrs. James—but I think Jenny was troubled about something."

"About what?"

He lifted his shoulders and let them drop. "She refused to tell me. I think she had had a letter from someone here. When I asked her, she told me that it was something private, that she could take care of."

"Dear me! But you don't think this had to do with her father?"

"No, I do not. I tell you why—because when I asked her what she was frightened of, she changed the subject. And the subject to which she changed it was—her father."

"Ah, yes. That makes a great deal of sense."

"I am glad to hear you say so."

"Tell me. I—ah—I don't wish to be indelicate, Mr. Ponseca, but—"

Ponseca smiled and his eyes lit up. "No, Mrs. James. Jenny Riley and I were close friends. Nothing more." He shook his head. "It was not for want of trying, on my part, that we remained so."

"Er—naturally not," said Dewey, doing her best to sound worldly.

"But she was very wise, that young girl. She knew the kind of man I am—restless. I cannot help that my heart is a big one, and that women delight me, more than any other power on this earth. More, even, than my dancing. I am faithful, in my heart, to many women."

"Always true, in your fashion?"

"That is it, precisely, Mrs. James." He leaned forward and looked deeply into her eyes. "I am not surprised to find you a sophisticated woman. I can always sense such things about a beautiful lady." He looked at her, smiling. "I do not embarrass you, I hope?"

"Er, no—not at all, Mr. Ponseca." Dewey shifted uncomfortably under his gaze.

"You see, I also know that such beauty as you possess tells that your heart is absolutely faithful. My style of loving is not for everyone. It is not for you. You love but one man."

Dewey firmly changed the subject. "Mr. Ponseca—tell me. If Jenny was not in love with you, was there someone else?"

Ponseca leaned back and stared off to the far end of the garden, where a cardinal had begun to sing. He was quiet for a long time; then at last he spoke.

"Jenny, of course, had many suitors. Recently I believe she had had a brief fling with someone new. But I always felt there was something more for her—someone that had gone out of her life, in a painful way. He had left her, I think. She was very quiet about it. But I could tell that her affection for this person was very deep."

Dewey's mind flew instantly to Tommy Jones. "Was this person someone she had loved for a long time?"

"Oh, yes. I think she had loved him all her life."

"But he left her, you say."

"I thought so. She grew so sad at times that I didn't know how to help her. But she would not discuss it with me."

"You make her sound like a rather secretive young lady."

"Oh—Mrs. James. There are many ways to be secretive. Jenny held her secrets for her own reasons—not to be powerful, if you understand me."

"I do, indeed," said Dewey.

"No—she was private. And the man who had broken her heart, I think she feared for him, and yet was happy."

"She was afraid *for* him? Not *of* him, but *for* him?"

"Yes. I think she felt that his life was in her hands."

"Yes. I see. Mr. Ponseca—is there anyone here in town whom you knew before coming here?"

Ponseca's eyes flashed. "You refer, perhaps, to the swiftness of my growing friendship with Señora Ambler?"

"No, actually I don't. I wondered if there was someone else here in town that you or Jenny might have known from New York."

He shook his head. "I did not, of course, meet anyone in town on Saturday. But—I should think not. Jenny, of course, knew them all."

"Yet there is someone here who, I am sure, knows you. Or at least, I had the impression that he might have known Jenny. He is a dancer, like yourself."

Ponseca shook his head. "I am sorry. If I should recall anything, I will certainly inform you. But for now, no."

"Well. Thank you, Mr. Ponseca," said Dewey, rising. He stood and took her hand, then bowed over it.

"It is my very great pleasure, indeed, Mrs. James, to spend time with so charming a woman."

Dewey headed back out through the lounge, where a tempest was brewing. A young girl, dressed in a chambermaid's outfit, was protesting loudly to the manager. "I didn't do it," she said. "Honest, Mr. Randolph, I didn't. That room was perfect when I made it up, and nobody's been in it since."

Mr. Randolph, a rounding, balding man in his forties, shook his finger at the young woman. "Don't you lie to me, girl. I suppose you think you're clever, don't you?"

Good heavens, thought Dewey as she headed out into the growing darkness outside. This town is coming apart at the seams.

14

WHILE DEWEY WAS discussing love with Alejandro Ponseca, Fielding Booker was fuming. He sat behind his desk, staring out the tiny window into the alley behind police headquarters. The inactivity was infuriating—the more so because he knew that it was absurd.

"Fenton!" he bellowed at last.

"Yessir," said Sergeant Mike Fenton, appearing swiftly at his superior's office door.

"Mikey, we've got to lick this thing."

"Yessir."

"Now, I know, and you know, that any suspicion of my guilt is crazy." He looked at his sergeant sharply. "Don't we?"

"Yes, sir. Of course."

"Well then. How do you explain the pretty pickle we're in here?"

"Uh, sir, it's Mrs. Ambler."

"I know who's behind it, Mikey. What I want to know is why. Henrietta Ambler thinks she owns this town. And George Farnham, confound his political little soul, has rolled over for her. But I won't sit back and watch this investigation go down the drain. You understand me?"

"Yes, sir."

"Good. Have a seat."

Fenton pulled up a chair and attended.

"The first thing we have got to get to the bottom of is that dancing fellow, Mike."

"Ponseca."

"That's the one." Booker leaned comfortably back in his chair and smiled. "Henrietta Ambler may think she has put a spoke in my wheels, but nobody says I can't keep the peace in my own town, do they?"

"No, sir," said Fenton warily.

"That's right, they don't. So. First thing I want is a background check on that fellow. I don't like the looks of him. And I didn't like the way Henrietta Ambler looked at him, either, on Saturday night. If I didn't know her for a cold-hearted you-know-what, Mikey, I'd swear she'd fallen for the man."

"Yes, sir."

"And you know what I think, Mike?"

"No, sir, I don't."

"I think Henrietta Ambler is covering up for her Latin lover. Hey? What do you say to that?"

"It's certainly a possibility, sir."

"Possibility? Hah! Why else would she involve herself? She's not interested in Jenny Riley—that girl could have been a flea on a dog, for all that Henrietta Ambler cares about her."

"Yes, sir, I see your point."

"Good. I thought you would. So. I think it's time we looked after the interests of the richest lady in Hamilton. Get that man's name and description on the wire. I want a full accounting of his birth, parents, college—if any, which I doubt—wife or wives—and you can bet, my boy, that there's more than one wife, eh?"

"Sir."

"And everything else about him. My hunch is that he killed that girl. She must have known something about his shady past. Threatened to tell Mrs. Ambler—spoil his chances with the richest woman in town. The battle lines are drawn, Mike. We're going to dig it all up and lay it out for the great lady of Leithdown Farm. Teach her to stick her nose in police business."

"Right away, sir. Anything else?"

"No. Run along."

"Yes, sir."

Fielding Booker began to feel much better. Let them try to pin his wings. They would see—when it came to crimes on his turf, Fielding Booker was the man for the job.

"Well, my dear? How do you like this peasant fare?"

Dewey was at George Farnham's kitchen table, tucking in to a skillfully prepared cassoulet. It was well known in Hamilton that George was a magnificent cook; and in recent months he had taken to cooking supper for Dewey regularly. Some of the wags in town thought that he was trying to win her heart this way; which may well have been true. Certainly, he had gone beyond merely showing off in the kitchen. Making dinner for Dewey was usually the high point of the week for George.

"The cassoulet is marvelous, George. But you and I shouldn't be eating such rich food."

"Nonsense, Dewey. Hardy country folk have been eating cassoulet for centuries with no ill effects whatsoever. I challenge you to name one civilization that has flourished on a steady diet of oat bran."

Dewey smiled. "The Houyhnhnms, of course."

"The who?"

"In *Gulliver's Travels*."

"Oh. Giants, were they?"

"No, George. The giants were the Brobdingnagians. The Houyhnhnms were horses."

"Ah. Now I follow you."

"They were the only reasonable creatures that Lemuel Gulliver encountered. Had a very cultivated, peaceful society."

"That was only a book. Eat your dinner, Dewey. And tell me what you've found out."

Dewey shook her head. "I think I'm falling down on the job, George. I went to see Alejandro Ponseca this afternoon, hoping to get some kind of insight into Jenny's New York life."

"And?"

"There wasn't much he could tell me. I think he adored her, but she kept her private life private. But he did tell me that something seemed to be worrying her about coming home."

"Her father?"

Dewey shook her head. "Definitely not her father. Something else."

"Strange. She really cut her ties to Hamilton when she left."

"It occurred to me it might be something to do with Tommy Jones."

"Now, Dewey . . ."

"Honestly, George. Just because you never liked the boy, you think that the rest of the world has forgotten him. I don't think Jenny forgot him."

"What makes you say that?"

"Mr. Ponseca seemed to think that Jenny's heart had been broken, but that she still loved the one responsible. If I were a young woman in love with a man who was having a nervous breakdown, I'm sure my heart would break, too."

George shook his head firmly. "I don't think so, Dewey. That's not the impression I got the other day from Mildred Jones."

"When?"

"I told you. I ran into her at the grocery store. And she was caustic in the extreme about Jenny Riley. Said that she was completely caught up in her success—selfish and self-satisfied. I got the impression that she had abandoned Tommy Jones."

Dewey's mind flashed back to the scene at the River Festival on Saturday, when Jenny Riley had made her entrance. She remembered vividly the look of contempt on Mildred Jones's face. "Yes, I think that Mildred did feel that way. But, George—how do we know that Mildred is right about Jenny?"

"Hmmm. You think she might not be?"

"Well, my goodness. She seems to be the only one who thinks so. Did you and Jack talk about Jenny?" George had spent part of the afternoon with Jack Riley.

"Yes, we did. He showed me that last letter that Jenny

had written to him." George looked sad. "He's not used to all this attention, you know. It's very hard on him."

"I can imagine it is. What did Jenny's letter say?"

"It was very sweet—a long letter, telling him how thrilled she was to be coming home at last. She said that she hoped the past was behind them, and that he would learn to be proud of her in time."

"Nothing about Tommy?"

George shook his head.

Dewey ate thoughtfully. "And what about that horrible Norman Fox, George?"

"Hmm? What about him?"

"Do you know—I think he wanted to speak to Jenny that night. Right after Delphine slapped him and marched off the dance floor."

"Dewey, you have an obsession about that man."

"No, I don't," she countered firmly. "You couldn't see what I saw. He walked over to her table—to Jenny's table. Then he seemed to change his mind and went off in another direction."

"Probably couldn't get through the crowd."

Dewey shook her head. "No. It wasn't that." Dewey sighed heavily. "Poor Bookie," she said.

George nodded. "He's fit to be tied. But we'll clear this thing up, between us, Dewey."

Dewey smiled. "As long as we can somehow trick Bookie into thinking he solved the case."

"That shouldn't be difficult."

"No," said Dewey with a laugh.

15

DEWEY SPENT TUESDAY morning at the library. She had almost forgotten about Professor Renfrew and was distressed to see him turn up shortly after she had opened up for business. She shook her head. Perhaps the time had come to speak to somebody about Tom Campbell. His snobbery was bad enough; Dewey usually managed to ignore him. But to have invited this ghoul into their midst was almost unforgivable. Dewey forced herself to be courteous.

"Good morning, Dr. Renfrew," she said brightly as the man made his way to the circulation desk.

"Oh, good morning, Mrs. James," he said with a polite nod. "And how are you today?"

"Very well, thank you."

"Glad to hear it. Your Mr. Campbell has persuaded me to use the library for my writing for the next few days. There is quite a lot of noise at the inn, you know."

"Is there? I've always thought it such a peaceful place."

"There seems to have been some kind of to-do about that young woman's room. Don't ask me what it's all about. But with the police tramping through, and the manager shouting at his staff, the Hamilton Inn is not conducive to my researches. You haven't let this foolishness upset your routine at the library, I see. Quite wise."

"Well, one must carry on," she replied lamely.

"I understand that the police have not yet made an arrest in this matter." He shook his head. "Foolish of them even to try, you know. Some things are best left alone."

Dewey was shocked. "Surely, Professor, you can't expect them to sit idle when there is a murderer on the loose."

He smiled enigmatically. "Perhaps this was a necessary death, Mrs. James. Appeasement is never an easy or painless matter."

"Oh, good heavens, you don't mean that."

"Don't I?" His spectacles shone back at her; she couldn't read his eyes. "At any rate, if someone thinks that police captain had anything to do with it, I'd say they are being rather thick. Wouldn't you?"

"I most certainly would," she agreed fervently. "I've known Fielding Booker for nearly half a century."

"Yes—although I suppose every murderer has friends from childhood. But you know, he wasn't the only person to visit that young lady's dressing room."

Good heavens! thought Dewey. She had completely forgotten that Professor Renfrew had even attended Saturday's festivities. Was there something that he had witnessed?

"Do you mean to say, Professor, that you saw someone else going into Jenny's dressing room?"

"Oh, yes," he replied mildly. "The fellow with the rug."

"Norman Fox?"

"Don't know his name. The one that left the dance floor in such a hurry. While the competition was going on."

"Norman Fox," said Dewey.

"If you say so, yes," agreed the professor.

"Professor Renfrew—this is important. What time was it that you saw Norman Fox visiting Jenny's dressing room?"

"I couldn't say, my dear lady."

"Was it before he left the dance floor?"

"Oh, good gracious, no. It was shortly before the performance." He regarded Dewey with a skeptical, amused air. "I can sense that this information appeals to you in some way."

"Well, my heavens, Professor. It might lead to discovering who committed the murder."

"That I very much doubt. But if you feel that the police are determined to interfere in this little matter—which, mind you, would be a *very* dangerous course of action— then perhaps someone ought to ask him about it."

"Now, Mr. Ponseca, if you please, sir. A woman is dead. And your efforts at protesting your innocence—charming though they are—will get you nowhere." Booker glowered across the desk in the interrogation room at Alejandro Ponseca. The dancer's composure had not deserted him, not even after two solid hours of questioning by the fearsome Fielding Booker.

"I tell you, Captain, that I had no hand in this grisly affair. If you stubbornly refuse to believe in my attachment to Jenny, perhaps you will incline to the cynical viewpoint."

"I have already done so, sir. You were alone on that gallery with Jenny Riley for a full quarter of an hour before the performance began; and again directly after the floor show was over. You are the only person, Mr. Ponseca, who had access to that poor girl's dressing room."

"But, Captain. Really. Look at the facts. Jenny was my dear friend. And—what may be more important, from the point of view of this tragedy—she was my livelihood. It was she, it was Jenny Riley, who filled the audience night after night, there on Broadway. And here, too, in Hamilton. You must see that. To kill Jenny would be to shoot myself in the foot—quite literally. I do assure you."

"Hmmm," grumbled Booker. "There is no need for you to teach the police their business, Mr. Ponseca. We have found the bottle that contained the nicotine sulfate, you know."

"Oh?"

"Yes, indeed. And you had better believe me, sir, that as soon as we trace it to its point of purchase, we shall have enough evidence for a conviction. You just bear that it mind, sir." He leered at Ponseca.

"I am very glad to hear it, Captain. When you can find who purchased the poison, the shopkeeper will vindicate me. She or he will tell you that it was not I—no, it was not Alejandro Ponseca—who has bought the venom that snuffed the life from my darling Jenny Riley." He began quietly to cry.

"Mr. Ponseca!" shouted Booker. Fielding Booker was an old-fashioned, hard-boiled, all-American male. The sight of another man in tears turned his stomach like nothing else on earth. "Will you kindly stop your blubbering? For the love of Pete." He stood, exasperated and deeply disgusted, as Ponseca blew his nose. "You may go, sir, for the moment. But I warn you that you are not to leave town. I will not stand for it. Do I make myself understood?"

"On my honor as a gentleman," said Ponseca, rising, "I will stay to see this thing to the bitter, bitter end. It is the least I can do, for Jenny's sacred memory." He departed. Booker watched him go with abhorrence. Crying! Like a bloody baby. He shook his head and padded slowly back to his office. Once behind his desk he stared out the window. How that marvelous girl could have been involved with such a man! Booker thought about Jenny Riley—her sleepy blue eyes, her long neck, her remarkable spine. Without warning there was an unfamiliar sensation in his eyes and nose; a tingling, as though he had sniffed straight ammonia. "Fenton!" he bellowed, warding it off. He reached for his hat and his walking stick.

"Sir." Fenton took a good look at his captain. The use of the walking stick usually spelled trouble, in one way or another. The old man only resorted to its comfort in the most extreme circumstances.

"Fenton. We are going to get that man. Do you understand me?"

"Yessir. We will."

"Good. Put Shoemaker on that bottle business. Tell her to check with every garden supply store within a fifty-mile radius. If that turns up nothing, tell her to get on the horn to mail-order outfits. Then New York City. We'll trace that poison."

"Sir."

"Then tell Machen I want every crumb of information on

that man. Credit cards, friends, enemies—you name it. You mind the fort. I'm going out. And if Mrs. Ambler calls, you tell her politely but firmly to go to hell. Got it?"

"Yes, sir."

16

FROM THE LIBRARY it was just a block or so to the tiny brick building that served as Hamilton's police headquarters. It was there that, with many misgivings, Dewey bent her steps at lunchtime.

In the thirty years that Dewey's husband had been chief of police in town, the placid building—with its ancient metal desks and well-worn file cabinets, its bad lighting, musty offices, and two usually vacant cells—had been a familiar haunt. But after Brendan James's death, it had taken Dewey several years to brave her fears and her longing, and enter the office once more. She had gone to help Fielding Booker in a murder investigation in which the life of a friend had been at stake; nothing less could have impelled her.

When she had at last taken that step, however, it was easy once more to feel at home there, and Dewey's visits became more frequent. The familiarity of the place, so unsettling on that first time back, was now again welcome. She had become an old hand at it.

It was a good thing, too, for Fielding Booker. Dewey James had helped him out of one tight spot after another; and although she set his teeth on edge, with her unorthodox manner and her intuitions about evidence, he had been forced to admit that she often had a point. Booker was very fond of his late captain's widow, despite her slightly dotty manner and her constant curiosity about police business. He had come to regard her sallies into his domain with mingled apprehension, amusement, and exasperation. In the end (although he never could admit it), he was usually glad that she had come.

Dewey was well aware of the effect she had on Captain Booker. You couldn't blame him, really. He was only trying to do his job in the best way he knew how. It was just that, occasionally, he missed the boat. Luckily, Dewey was sometimes there, ready with her idiosyncratic lifeline.

The circumstances of today's visit, however, were particularly tricky. She was certain that Booker would be in no mood to discuss the case with her—nor, indeed, with anyone. But she hoped to find a way to talk a few things over with Sergeant Fenton. Mike Fenton, Dewey knew, rather liked her.

"Mrs. James!" said that amiable young sergeant, as Dewey pushed open the door. "Welcome." He strode to the door and held it open for her, then leaned over to whisper conspiratorially. "Come to give the Big Cheese some advice?" he asked.

Dewey smiled wistfully. "Hello, Mike. I thought I might just stop in to see how everyone is faring. I—well, everyone in town is concerned, you know. How is the captain taking this situation?"

Fenton looked grim. "Maybe it's a lesson in wearing your heart on your sleeve. But if you wanted to talk to the captain, you've missed him. He's stepped out for a moment."

"Oh?" Dewey asked with interest. "Has he got a lead in the case?"

Fenton shrugged. "Don't know for sure, ma'am. I suspect," he added in a lower tone, "that he may have stopped in briefly at the Seven Locks."

"Oh, my. That bad? Well, never mind. *In vino veritas*, you know."

"Ma'am?"

"In wine there is truth, Mike. Never mind—I was actually rather hoping to have a word with you, if you can spare me a minute."

"Absolutely. This way." He held open a small gate in the

counter that divided the entryway from the main room. "Would you like some coffee?"

"Yes, thank you."

"Kate!" Fenton called. A pretty young policewoman appeared from the other end of the hallway. "Coffee for Mrs. James, please."

"Yes, sir," said Kate Shoemaker.

Fenton and Dewey settled in at his desk in the far corner of the big room. "So you've heard the rumors," he said.

"Yes—well, naturally—it's the talk of the town." She smiled as Kate Shoemaker brought a mug of coffee. "Thank you, Officer Shoemaker."

"That will be all, Kate," said Fenton firmly.

"Yes, sir," said Kate Shoemaker. She departed.

"Anyway," Dewey went on, "I have just had an interesting conversation with Professor Renfrew—you know, the human sacrifice man."

"Oh, yeah—Tom Campbell's buddy."

"That's the one." Dewey nodded and leaned forward. "He told me that he saw someone up on the gallery shortly before the performance began. And I thought, of course, that you ought to know about it at once. And—as he seemed disinclined to come to the police himself . . ." She smiled hopefully.

"Uh, yes, ma'am. Appreciate it." Fenton was suddenly glad the captain was out of the office. Booker was in a temper today, no doubt about it. So far the police inquiry into Alejandro Ponseca's background had drawn a blank. A full seven hours of grilling—first by Booker, then by Fenton, and again this morning by Booker—had not shaken the man's story. He claimed only to have been changing in his own dressing room when he heard some kind of cry from the room next door. He rushed to Jenny's room and found her collapsed on the floor, breathing her last. But Booker was determined to nail Ponseca. The captain wouldn't take kindly, just at present, to suggestions that might distract him from his goal. "Gee, ma'am, I suppose you ought to tell us about it. I'm sure the captain will want to know. Who is it?"

"The man who teaches dance at the In-Time School. Norman Fox."

"Hmm," said Sergeant Fenton.

"And you know, it had occurred to me that he might know Jenny in some way—be connected to her in some way. They were both dancers in New York, you see."

"You mean he knew her?"

"Well, I'm not certain of that. But, don't you see, Mike? He may very well have important information about this business."

"Just at present, Mrs. James—"

"Unless, of course, you are following up other leads right now?"

"I really couldn't say, Mrs. James. I'm afraid that's confidential police information."

"Yes, Mike. I quite understand. I only hope you're not wasting valuable time. That is to say—I hope that Captain Booker hasn't got it into his head that he needs to teach Mrs. Ambler any sort of lesson." She looked at him shrewdly.

"Of course not." Fenton was discomfited. He didn't like the thought of lying to Mrs. James—and if he hadn't been afraid of the wrath of Fielding Booker, he might well have been tempted to try the police theory out for her, to see what she thought of it. But that would be a very foolhardy course for a young sergeant with two small children. "We'll certainly look into it, Mrs. James." Fenton hoped he sounded noncommittal.

"Oh, Mike—you think I'm crazy, don't you?"

"No, no—honest, Mrs. James. Not at all." He smiled and leaned forward, clasping his hands together on the desk. Perhaps he could just give her a small hint. Dewey James was a pretty sharp old lady. "I—uh—I know you kind of have a nose for these things. It's just that, uh, right now, Captain Booker is pretty sure that—"

"What's that you say, Mike?" bellowed Fielding Booker. He had stolen in quietly through the front door. Dewey wondered how long he had been listening to them.

"Hello, Bookie," said Dewey cheerfully, twisting around in her chair to wave at him.

"Hello, Dewey." Fielding Booker sounded resigned. "Well, well. What brings you here today? No"—he held up a hand—"don't tell me, let me guess. You've come to organize the police library for us."

"Well, not exactly, Bookie." She might as well brazen it out. "You see—"

"No? Pity. We could use an organizing hand in here. Just look." He gestured to a small bookshelf on a far wall, which sagged unevenly under the weight of several telephone books. "Let us know when you get the time, eh, Dewey? Or, better yet, don't call us. We'll call you. Hah-hah." Booker glared at his sergeant. "Fenton. I'll see you in my office right away."

"Yessir." He sprang to his feet and looked apologetically at Dewey. "Sorry, Mrs. James—duty calls."

"That's quite all right, Mike." Then she whispered conspiratorially, "Just you let me know if my little idea is of any use to you."

"Sure will, Mrs. James."

17

It was a measure of Dewey's devotion to Fielding Booker that she never allowed herself to be turned aside by his stubbornness. In all of Hamilton no one had a more durable reputation for stubbornness than Fielding Booker. Dewey held out little hope that her suggestion to Mike Fenton would be followed up; it was not as if she had any facts to present. Clearly, she would have to make a few discreet inquiries on her own. She returned to the library and, as she reshelved books, she thought through her plan.

She was of the opinion that Needham Renfrew was entirely out of his mind. On the other hand, she thought to herself, "great wits are sure to madness near allied"; and vice versa. Perhaps he had seen Norman Fox paying a visit to Jenny's dressing room. There was very little reason for him to concoct such a story out of thin air, especially when he had expressed his indifference to seeing the killer brought to justice. Was that indifference to be believed?

She carefully reconstructed the scene at the Great Hall. Renfrew had been sitting somewhere near the right-hand side of the audience; from that vantage point, she imagined, he would have a fairly clear view of the far side of the gallery.

The more she thought it through, the more convinced Dewey became that there might be some connection between Fox and Jenny Riley. Her mind flashed back to the scene when Fox had left the dance floor that night. There had been something odd about the way he swerved to avoid Jenny Riley's table. Fox had moved to Hamilton from New

York six months ago; the world of professional ballroom dancing couldn't be all that large, she reasoned. And if he had been seen going up the stairs to the dressing rooms, there was probably some connection there. In any event, it wouldn't hurt to inquire, just a little.

As soon as her morning chores were complete, Dewey made a hasty excuse to Tom Campbell and betook herself down the hill, toward the river, and once more into the In-Time School of Ballroom Dance.

"Anybody home?" she called out as she reached the top of the stairs and the depressing emptiness of the dance studio.

"Be right there!" Norman Fox replied. Dewey stepped in and looked around. She could hear Fox's voice coming from a small office off on the right. He was on the telephone; she pricked up her ears.

"That's right. Be here at eleven o'clock, or your ass is grass, man." Goodness! thought Dewey. Norman Fox was a most unpleasant young man. As he slammed down the receiver, she adopted an air of meek patience.

"Mrs. James!" said Norman Fox, his voice heavy with mock delight as he hastily pulled on a brown sports coat. "How good to see you. What can I do for you today?"

"Hello, Mr. Fox. Well. You see—I had *such* fun here the other day, and I thought perhaps that you might be able to fit me in for those private lessons you mentioned."

"Whoa, Nellie," said Fox. "I mean—we'd be pleased to schedule you, but I don't think *you* need our lessons, Mrs. James. You looked pretty good out there the other night."

"Thank you," said Dewey, trying her best to look at once suitably proud and diffident. "But you know, at my age these things are not as easy as they used to be. I was positively exhausted after the dancing, you know. My one consolation," she added with bright innocence, "is that I wasn't the only one who seemed tired by the end of the cha-cha." She smiled up at him.

"Yes, well—"

"And I just *know* that with practice I could build up my

stamina. The idea of a *real* night on the town leaves me tired just thinking of it."

"Does it, now?"

"Yes. And you know, I have a—a friend, a most generous friend, who lives in New York and has invited me to come as—as his guest. Do you know, he said he wants to take me dancing! At the Rainbow Room in Rockefeller Center." She blushed becomingly. Dewey always blushed when she spoke an outright lie; it was sometimes a useful shortcoming. "And I did *so* want to be able to live up to his expectations."

"I get the picture," said Norman Fox. "A little romance, hey-hey?" He took Dewey's arm and ushered her into the office. Obviously, thought Norman Fox with glee, Delphine didn't know what she was talking about. This old bat was a pushover. "Well, now. Let me think. How about a package of six private lessons? We could work on those *basic* building blocks that we touched on the other night, develop your tone, and make it easier for you all around. And when *I* have finished with you, you'll be in terrific shape for your *main* man. Sound good?"

"Oh, yes—yes, indeed."

"Great. Suppose you just have a seat, Mrs. James."

Dewey sat, and Norman Fox went to his desk and opened a large ledger book. "First things first. When is this big trip to the Big Apple, eh?"

"Oh—in three weeks' time."

"Three weeks—we'll have to have a crash course, Mrs. James. What time of day would suit you best?"

"Anytime, really. I'm really more or less retired, you know, from the library, and I can arrange my schedule to suit whatever openings you may have."

"That's fine." He browsed through the ledger, making notes on a slip of paper.

"You're a New Yorker, aren't you, Mr. Fox?"

"Yep."

"I ask, you know, because I thought it was so tragic about Jenny Riley. Was she a close friend of yours?"

He shook his head, keeping his eyes fixed on the ledger book. "Nope."

"But still, it must have been nice to see her again. You *did* pay a visit to her dressing room, on the night of the performance, I think."

Fox looked at her levelly. "Where did you hear that?"

"Well—my goodness, Mr. Fox. There were more than two hundred people there that night. Naturally, one of them was bound to see you going up those stairs."

"Yeah? Well—Mrs. James, I hate to disappoint you. But I didn't know Jenny Riley. And I certainly didn't go to see her in her dressing room."

"Oh, dear me. My mistake."

"Don't let it worry you."

"I just assumed, you see, that, being a dancer, you might have been her friend."

"Yeah—well, lotta dancers out there, Mrs. James. Jenny was a star. Not me. I'm in this rack—the business for the sheer pleasure of teaching people like you."

"Oh, I see. I hope you find it gratifying, then."

"Yeah." Fox wondered briefly if his denials sounded curt. "Well, of course, I knew who she was. She got around, Jenny Riley, before she hit it big. Danced with a lot of different companies in the city. But I never actually met her."

"A pity you didn't get the chance to meet her the other night, then."

"Yeah—well. That's how it goes."

"So it does. It's so sad that she died here. Her father, you know, is terribly distressed."

"Oh, yeah? I heard she and her old—her father didn't get along too well."

"Oh, you know how parents and children can be. I'm sure there was nothing to that rumor."

Norman Fox finished writing out Dewey's schedule. He tore off a piece of paper and handed it to her. "Unfortunately, Mrs. James, since you didn't sign up for your lessons last week, I can't give you the special discount. It was for last week only."

"Oh, dear me," said Dewey.

"But," he added, "since you came to the group lesson as a guest of someone else, it's just like getting seven lessons for the price of six. Am I right?"

"Oh, yes, I see. How kind of you to point that out, Mr. Fox. How much will the lessons cost?"

"It's a package deal. If you were to sign up one at a time, it would be three hundred dollars; but when you buy a package, you get a break. Two fifty."

"That sounds reasonable," said Dewey, hoping to find a way to wriggle out of this. For two hundred and fifty dollars she could fly to California to see her daughter, Grace.

"Here you go. Six lessons: three times a week for two weeks. Okay?" He handed her a long, preprinted contract.

"Marvelous, Mr. Fox. Thank you very much."

Dewey picked up her handbag.

"Uh—could you sign the contract, Mrs. James? That way we can get all the paperwork taken care of, and we'll be sure you won't miss out on anything."

"Oh, my—yes, Mr. Fox. The thing is, I'm rather forget-ful, you know, and I've left my reading glasses behind. I never sign anything I haven't read *very* carefully. I'm old-fashioned that way. I'll take it home with me and review it, and bring it along in the morning, if that will suit you."

Dewey folded the paper very carefully and tucked it away in a spare envelope in her handbag.

Norman Fox was stuck. "That will be perfectly fine," he said, cursing inwardly.

"Well, then. Good-bye, Mr. Fox."

That afternoon, as she worked in her garden, Dewey James was deeply dissatisfied. Her efforts at investigation—meager as they had been—had led her nowhere; and although she did not for a moment think that Fielding Booker had poisoned Jenny's drink (absurd notion!), she was forced to concede that she hadn't lit on any other solution. She was more than a little inclined to suspect Norman Fox of dirty dealings; the more so after she had looked at the fine print on the In-Time contract. But she had showed her hand; somehow, she was rather certain that Norman Fox had smelled a rat. She would have to see what the police came up with about Norman Fox.

Or would she? Dewey turned over some earth in her perennial border and pondered. If Norman Fox didn't know Jenny, how was it that he knew about her quarrel with her father?

And—come to think of it—how was it that Jenny Riley had been persuaded to come to the Hamilton Homecoming at all?

Dewey dropped her trowel and dashed inside the house to phone Susan Miles.

"Susan, it's Dewey."

"Hi, Dewey."

"My dear—have you still got the correspondence files for the Homecoming?"

"Sure. They're in a heap in the den—in fact, Nick is threatening to move out until I can dispose of them."

"Wonderful. I'll be right there."

Susan and Nick Miles lived just a few miles from Dewey, on the other side of Adams Hill. She was there in minutes.

"What's this all about, Dewey?" asked Susan.

Dewey looked at Susan's two little girls. Susan took the hint. "Meg, Elizabeth, you two run outside and play for a while." They departed, giggling mysteriously. "Dewey?"

"I'm not sure, precisely. And I don't want to get ahead of myself. Where are the files?"

"In the den." Susan led the way to a cozy back room, where a coffee table was piled high with papers and envelopes. "Dewey, does this have something to do with Jenny's death?"

"I think it may," Dewey replied thoughtfully. "What we need to find, Susan, is a copy of the committee's letter to Jenny—the form letter, inviting her to come. Was she one of the people on your list?"

Susan Miles shook her head. "No—but here are the lists. We can easily find out who did have her."

Dewey and Susan pored over the lists of names and

addresses that had been assigned to the various committee members. They had been divided alphabetically; George Farnham had the *R*s. But Jenny Riley's name did not appear on his list, nor on any of them.

"How strange!" said Susan. "I don't get it, Dewey. Somebody did send her an invitation. I wonder why she isn't here."

"Try to recall, Susan—did you perhaps ask someone to write to her, but not jot it down?"

Susan Miles shook her head slowly. "I don't think so. I don't remember, anyway, if I did. I do remember the day we got her response. We were opening the letters in George's office—you remember, Dewey?"

Dewey nodded. The responses had all come to a post office box rented especially for the occasion. "Yes. Who else was there?"

Susan thought for a moment then counted out on her fingers. "You, me, George, Nils, and Bookie." Susan looked at Dewey. "Is this important?"

"I think perhaps it is. Susan—you must not say a word of this to anyone. Promise me?"

Susan nodded. "You think it has something to do with her death?"

"Yes, indeed. I most certainly do," replied Dewey James in a soft voice.

18

"GEORGE, THIS IS very important," said Dewey into the telephone. "Did you send her the letter—you know, the form letter that we sent to all the out-of-towners. Did you send it to Jenny Riley?"

"Certainly not, my dear. I only had about a dozen people on my list, and Jenny Riley wasn't one of them."

"George, I'm frightened."

"Now, Dewey—"

"Seriously. This is very strange. Somebody wanted to get that poor girl here. This whole thing was thought out well in advance, clearly."

"What makes you say that?"

"Because we got a response from her. Addressed to the Homecoming Committee. But Susan and I couldn't find who had sent her the invitation."

"Mmm. Have you taken a survey of the entire sample, my dear?"

"What on earth do you mean, George? You sound like a scientist."

"Simple. Have you checked to see that the name of everyone else who replied was on those lists?"

"Well, no. But no one else was murdered, George. I see your point, but we are trying to find the truth here, not take an accurate sample of the population."

"So we are. Well—it's worth looking into, I think."

"I think so, too. The only problem is Bookie."

"Oh? You'd think he'd leap at the chance to find the murderer."

"Yes. Indeed, I fear he has already leaped, George. I stopped in there today and had a little chat with Mike Fenton. He didn't want to give the game away, but you know he's a fairly transparent young man."

"Yes, I would agree with you there. Hope he never gets assigned to undercover duty."

"Exactly. Well, I had a small piece of information to pass on. But I'm afraid Bookie's decided on his murderer, George. And now he's trying to collect the evidence."

"Who do you think he's hit on?"

"Judging from the amount of dodging that Mike Fenton did this afternoon, I'd say it's Alejandro Ponseca."

"Well, my dear. You have to admit it's a strong possibility. The obvious suspect, up there alone with her."

"He wasn't alone." She related what Renfrew had told her. "But I'm afraid that information fell on deaf ears."

"Hmm. So he's going after Ponseca, with no evidence and another suspect in clear view of his sights. Even Bookie couldn't be that single-minded."

"Well, I'm not so sure about that, George. And you know, if you twist the situation round and round enough, you can probably make rather a complex fiction out of the whole."

"Yes, I suppose you're right. And Bookie's a powerfully inventive fellow when he wants to be."

"Isn't it true."

"Well. What's your plan, my dear?"

"I think I should have a talk with Jack Riley. Perhaps he would know who sent Jenny the letter."

"Mmmm."

"I know, George. That's why I called you. I have several errands to take care of, but I'll be through about five o'clock or so. Could you meet me at Jack's place?"

"I have a better idea," said George. "Why don't you swing by my place for a little supper? I'll make sure Jack is there."

"Thank you, George." Dewey knew that she could always count on George to cook dinner in a pinch. "Lovely. Six o'clock?"

"See you then."

* * *

Dewey finished up with the perennial border and looked at her watch. She would just have time to bathe and get to Winchester's—the local nursery—before going to George's house. She needed to see about some azaleas that Abby Scott was getting in for her. And she could hardly be accused of meddling if she happened to ask one or two questions of a neighbor, in the course of her day. There was an idea that Dewey wished to explore.

Winchester's Nursery was a sprawling concern, a supplier of every kind of perennial, annual, shrub, and tree imaginable. Abby Scott had always been a keen gardener, and she took obvious pleasure in her work at Winchester's. As she drove up the long road that bisected a tiny forest of fir seedlings, Dewey thought about what Susan Miles had said the other day. Could it be that the Scotts were running out of money? Alfred Scott's investments were said to have done fairly well, but Dewey had seen with her own eyes Alfred Scott driving a Ford compact. Something dire must have prompted him to sell his Mercedes. Perhaps the Scotts did rely on Abby's income from this job. Perhaps Alfred was gambling again, after all.

It was absurd, of course—with Henrietta Ambler, the wealthiest person in all of Hamilton, not five miles away. Surely there had been some kind of settlement on Abby when her father died—but then again, perhaps not. Kent Ambler had never seemed to be able to get around his wife. Dewey could easily imagine that Henrietta had put her foot down in the matter of inheritance. And it was common knowledge that Henrietta Ambler detested Alfred Scott. It would be very like her to cut her daughter off from the family fortune simply because she had married a weak-minded man.

"Hello, Abby," said Dewey as she climbed out of the car and approached the potting shed.

"Hi, Mrs. James. How are you?"

"Very well, thank you. How are you? And Alfred?"

"We're fine, thanks. That is to say, I'm fine. I don't see

much of Alfred these days. He's always running off to meet with his publisher."

Dewey thought she detected some kind of strain in Abby Scott's voice. She wondered if Alfred's sudden and unexpected success had spoiled the balance of power in their marriage. "Oh, yes. The great novel. To tell you the truth, I had forgotten all about it."

Abby laughed. "Don't tell Alfred. You'll crush him. He's so thrilled, Mrs. James—Harbison House is sending him on a big road trip for publicity and everything. He spent all last night talking into a tape recorder so that he could hear what he'll sound like over the radio." They laughed. "Is there something I can do for you today? I was just closing up."

"Oh, dear. I won't keep you a second. I just thought I'd stop by and give you a check for those azaleas. Can they be delivered some time this week?"

"Sure thing. Come on around to the office." They made their way down a flagstone path through a huge convocation of shrubs, all sitting neatly at attention aboveground, handsome in their burlap jackets. "We've got some lovely lilacs, too. Can't I tempt you? There's a spot out in front of your house that just calls out for a lilac."

Dewey smiled and shook her head. "One project at a time for me, these days, I'm afraid."

"Okay—but if you change your mind, you let me know. I'll pick out the best of the bunch." They entered the small office, which doubled as a garden-supply store. Dewey looked around. They had obviously expanded since her last visit here. In one corner were elegant coffee-table books, displayed on sample patio furniture; against a far wall were a variety of tools and gadgets, all looking handmade, expensive, and English.

"Business looks to be going well," Dewey remarked kindly. "Fancy things you're selling."

"You know how it is, Mrs. James. Gardening is suddenly so stylish. We have to keep pace with our customers."

"Well, it promises to be a lovely spring," said Dewey cheerfully.

"It sure got off to a lousy start the other night."

"So it did. Were you and Jenny friends, Abby? You're about the same age."

"Used to be friends. But not anymore, really. She used to send me a card at Christmas, that kind of thing. Sent me and Alfred a bowl from Tiffany's for our wedding. But in the last couple of years she hasn't been in touch. Maybe her success went to her head."

"Oh, I don't think so. She seemed very pleased to see you both at the library the other night."

"Yeah—well, that might have been good politics. I had the feeling she didn't like us much anymore. For whatever reason. I was always trying to get Alfred to look her up when he went to New York, but it was hard. You know how men are about stuff like that."

"I do," agreed Dewey.

"Yeah. Anyway, Jenny pretty much cut her ties to Hamilton—I was surprised to hear that she was turning up for the Homecoming."

"Were you?"

Abby Scott nodded. "Sure. I feel bad, though, that I wasn't a better friend to her. Especially when we heard about Tommy. I wonder if he's even heard the news."

"Yes, I was thinking about that myself. Does anyone in town keep up with him?"

Abby shook her head. "I don't think so. Except old Mildred, of course. But she's crazy as a coot, so nobody ever wants to ask her about him. Every time the subject comes up, she goes off into a long tirade against 'Miss Jenny Riley.'" Abby looked momentarily sad. "I hope they catch this guy, Mrs. James."

"Yes, dear. So do I. The police are very hard at work on it, you know. They'll get to the bottom of it."

Abby Scott smirked. "If my mother would just let them get on with their job. I hear Captain Booker is having a fit. He's hardly the murdering type."

"I'm glad to hear you say that," said Dewey emphatically.

"But you know what La Grande Dame is like when she gets an idea into her head." Abby Scott smiled. "She's like a fancy dog with an expensive bone."

"Yes, Abby, I would have to agree with you there," replied Dewey. "Tell me—do you know what put this idea in her head in the first place?"

Abby nodded. "She's decided to be the avenging angel. You see, Mrs. James, I think she's fallen for that man. The dancer." She looked up at Dewey. "I notice that you're not scandalized by the idea," she said, smiling.

"Oh, heavens, no," replied Dewey. "I'm all for people finding true love wherever they can. No business of mine."

"No—but it is my business. At least, it should be. I never thought I'd see the day, Mrs. James, when I had to protect my mother. But that day seems to have arrived. I hope that Alejandro Ponseca hasn't got marriage on his mind."

"I hardly think he does, Abby," said Dewey, thinking back to her conversation with Ponseca. "I rather got the impression that he prefers to flit from flower to flower."

"Good," said Abby. "I wouldn't like to have to interfere."

As Abby Scott made out the invoice, Dewey regarded the shelves behind her, which were well stocked with a variety of plant foods, weed killers, growth enhancers, and pesticides. "Abby," said Dewey at last.

"Yes, Mrs. James?"

"I wonder—what would you recommend to someone who had a problem with aphids?"

"Ladybugs," replied Abby Scott firmly. She followed Dewey's glance to the shelves behind her. "We do carry pesticides. But I don't recommend them to my customers. Dangerous. Much better to work with nature, use the predators that are out there. Besides, ladybugs are good luck." She smiled and handed Dewey her receipt.

"Yes, so they are." Dewey wrote out her check and was on her way. As she drove down the long road into town, breathing in the fresh scent of the country air, she wondered deeply. Abby Scott probably knew that nicotine sulfate was the poison that had killed Jenny Riley. Did Abby Scott always recommend ladybugs to her customers? Or did she sometimes sell a nicotine preparation, for those really hard-to-eradicate pests?

And who had sent Jenny Riley the invitation to her own funeral?

19

As Dewey was writing out her check to Abby Scott, Fielding Booker was coming alive after his second Scotch at George Farnham's place.

"Well, at least it's a solid clue, Bookie," said George Farnham cheerily. "Say when."

"Just a splash, George. Thank you." Fielding Booker took the glass from Farnham and leaned back in his chair, sighing heavily. Farnham poured himself a drink and joined Booker at the kitchen table.

The sliding-glass doors to the riverbank out back were open, and the soft noises of the early spring evening drifted in on the mist.

"It is and it isn't, I'm afraid," Booker went on. "It's the first real lead we've had in this business, but it doesn't help." He shook his head and loosened his necktie. "Doesn't help me, anyway."

"Well, surely you can trace the bottle to its source."

"I thought so. But you know as well as I do, George, that there are a million garden-supply centers in this country. The thing could have come through some kind of mail-order outfit."

"Did you ask Rob Jensen?"

"First place young officer Shoemaker checked. Rob says he carries the stuff, but he hasn't sold a jar of it in upwards of three years. Jensen's a reliable man, wouldn't forget a thing like that. Nobody buys their garden supplies from him anymore, not since Abby Scott went to work at Winchester's."

116

"Have you talked to her?"

Booker nodded. "Sent young Machen over to have a word. But Abby says she doesn't stock this brand. Gave him an earful about the use of beneficial organics and predators, or some such guff." He pulled out a slip of paper from his breast pocket. " 'Aphids Away.' Stupid name for a product."

"Easy to buy, though, is it?"

"Used to be. Company seems to have gone out of business."

"Well, then, is that a help or a hindrance?"

"Blast it, man, what do you think?" Booker contemplated his drink sourly.

"Well, Bookie, is seems to me that if the poison wasn't purchased locally, that strengthens your case against Ponseca. That should be good news for you."

"It is, it is. I will happily hang that man. Teach Henrietta Ambler to spread rumors of corruption in the Hamilton force. Don't know why she's got this obsession about his innocence. Why does she care? That man turns my stomach. Do you know, he actually cried at headquarters today?"

"You don't say?"

"Damn foreigners. Come in here and stir everyone up. Get everybody thinking there's something wrong with *our* way of life."

"Oh, go on, Bookie. You sound like Doris Bock when you talk like that."

"Even Doris Bock is right some of the time, George." He sipped at his whiskey.

"Well. I haven't heard from Senator Davidson today, but I think I ought to tell you, Bookie, that he's mighty upset. He seems to be counting on Mrs. Ambler for this November's war chest."

"Politicians," said Booker with distaste. "Sell their own mothers for votes."

"I have to agree with you there—at least with regard to Gerald Davidson. I think you ought to know, Bookie, that he's talking about bringing in some kind of county or state supervisor on this case."

"I'm not surprised."

"But I think I've staved him off, for now. I—er, I more or less promised him, Bookie, that you had widened your field of suspects."

"Fine, fine, George. Let them think whatever they want. Just make sure that Henrietta Ambler keeps her fat nose out of my business. Women!"

"Speaking of women—Dewey's coming round here for a bite of supper tonight." He looked at the huge old clock on the wall. "Be here in about an hour. Care to stay?" George Farnham knew the risk was very small indeed that Booker would accept his invitation.

"Lord, George. You, too? I thought you were my friend." He polished off his drink, set his glass down with a bang, and donned his hat. "Exit, stage left."

Even in his youth, when there had been a chance that things would go right for him, Jack Riley had not been a particularly friendly or happy soul. As he grew older, he grew decidedly sour. Somehow, Jack Riley's life had gone off the rails. His wife had died when Jenny was just a small girl; and he had done his best with the child, but there had never been much happiness in their little twosome of a family. He was a strongly built man—or had been, before softness and beer had rounded him and dulled him. If he had lived in simpler times—a century before, when men were men—he would have prospered, done right by himself and his family. He had been born into the wrong century. Or so he had told himself, constantly, for twenty years.

But it was small wonder that Jack Riley had few friends in town. His manner was curt, often rude; and he sneered at the success of others as often as he made excuses for his own failure. The only reason that George Farnham had kept up any sort of friendship with him was simple; they sometimes fished together. Their occasional jaunts upriver in a boat, or farther away to lakes and other rivers, made a perfect basis for a particular kind of friendship; the focus

was always out *there*: on the water, on the fish, on the bait
and the lures and the weights; conversation was necessarily
brief. What was more, Jack was a fairly expert fisherman.
Far better than George Farnham—which was why Jack
liked George.

Jack Riley hadn't been invited out to dinner in so long
that he felt a little like a fraud when he turned up at George's
house at six o'clock. In his discomfort he was inclined to be
more rude than usual.

"So," he said flatly, downing his second beer and
plonking his mug down hard on George's kitchen table. "Is
this maybe a pity thing?"

"What's that?" asked George, who was at the enormous,
industrial-looking stove, measuring a few spoonfuls of
sherry into a large, heavy pot.

"This." Riley gestured around. "Me coming here for
dinner. You never invite me to dinner, George."

"You don't like to go out to dinner. You always complain
about the food," replied George good-naturedly. "Don't
want to get my feelings hurt, that's all."

"Yeah." Riley belched. "Well, what are we having,
anyway?"

"Stew."

"Stew? You ask me over for stew?"

"It's fancy French stew. You'll like it. It's one of my top
ten."

"Okay. Where's the beer?"

"Icebox. You don't mind helping yourself, do you,
Jack?"

"Nah." He rose sluggishly, planting his huge feet on the
ground and rising up like a tired, dry whale. "So your
girlfriend's coming, too, huh?" He slammed the icebox
door and shambled over to the stove, looking skeptically
down into George's stewpot. "What's in there?"

"Potatoes, carrots, onions, and venison."

"Venison? Like deer?"

"Sure thing."

"Venison." He crossed back to the table and descended
mightily into the chair once more. "How about that." There

was a hiss as he opened the beer bottle. "So. You didn't answer me."

"I didn't understand your question," replied George. "If you are asking me, Jack, if Dewey and I are courting, then you know that I am far too much of a gentleman to reply."

"Don't give me that junk. You and her are always together. Hell, man, if I know about it, it can't be much of a secret."

"If you know about it, Jack, then I don't see why you needed to ask." George grinned at him. "Come here and taste this. Tell me what it needs."

Riley did as he was told. "Salt. Needs salt."

George obliged with the salt shaker as the doorbell rang. He adjusted the flame and handed off the wooden spoon to Riley. "Stir." He went to let Dewey in at the front door.

"Hello, my dear," he said, planting a friendly kiss on her cheek. "So glad you could make it."

"Thank you, George," replied Dewey. "Something smells delicious."

"Jack is cooking up a storm," replied George with a wink. "Come on back." He led the way down the newly remodeled hall and into the bright, airy kitchen at the back of the house. Dewey sometimes wondered why George had even bothered to put in a living room when he had remodeled this old mill building. He was always happiest in his kitchen, with its high ceilings and the large sliding-glass doors giving out onto the river. He probably would never think of entertaining his friends anywhere else in the house.

"Hello, Jack," said Dewey.

"Evening," replied Riley. He had sat down again, but now he stumbled slowly to his feet, prodded by some elusive memory of the correct situational response.

"Jack, see what Dewey will have to drink, would you?" George set about preparing a salad.

"Oh—what is everyone else having?"

Riley raised his glass in answer.

"Beer. What a lovely idea. I think perhaps I'll join you."

As he shredded the lettuce for the salad, George smiled. Dewey was perfect.

When dinner was well under way, Dewey launched in to the subject. She had had plenty of time to think, over the course of the afternoon; but still it was ticklish going. Jack Riley was not inclined to be chatty on the simplest subjects; and on the subject of Jenny he had always been taciturn. But there were things Dewey wanted, very badly, to know.

"Jack," she said finally with a hope that she could strike the right note, "I was curious about something and hoped you could give me an answer."

"Doubt it." He reached for a piece of bread from the basket. "But go ahead."

"Well—the thing is this. You know how pleased we all are that Jenny could come for the Homecoming. It meant a great deal to us."

"Yeah. Sure."

"And you see—well, the thing is, that to have such a big star turn up in our midst was really, almost, surprising."

"You're telling me."

"And I thought perhaps that it was at your—encouragement, you know, that Jenny had decided to come home."

Jack Riley shook his head. "Nope. I would never've thought she'd come. Never came before."

"No. Which is why, frankly, I was curious."

"You mean it's weird, how she never came home once in twelve years, and then when she does come home she gets herself killed."

"Well, yes."

"Me, too."

"You, too, what, Jack?" asked George.

"I think it's weird. I think it's crazy. It's not like she forgot me or anything—she sent a lot of, well, presents my way in the last few years." He looked abashed. "And she knew I wasn't mad at her anymore. But I couldn't ask her to come and see her old man for no reason. Had to be a reason."

Dewey was momentarily nonplussed. If Jack Riley had sent the invitation, she would have to go back to the drawing board. "You mean to say, Jack, that you thought the Homecoming would be a good reason, and you told her about it?"

"Me? Hah. No." He looked sad for a moment. "Maybe I should've tried before. But I was waiting for a good reason. And I didn't think about the Homecoming as being anything, except maybe a time to get a little drunk or something. I would never've thought of asking Jenny to come."

"You didn't."

"Nope. She just wrote and said she was coming, was all. That she had been invited, she was gonna come."

"But she didn't mention anything about what reason—what particular reason—she may have had for coming home just now?"

Jack Riley shook his big head slowly. "Nope. Said a lot of stuff about her and me, how she hoped I would be proud. Like that."

Dewey thought hard. Jack Riley hadn't told Jenny about the Homecoming. "Jack, has there been anyone asking you, lately, about Jenny?"

"Whole damn town. All day and night. Police, too—and now you two. What is this?" Riley, opening a fourth beer, was well on his way to his nightly oblivion. "Huh? What is this?"

"What I meant, was, before Jenny's return. Jack—did anyone ask you for her address in New York?"

Riley shook his head. "Nope. Didn't need any address. Just write 'Jenny Riley, Star, care of Post Office.'"

"Did she mention, when she got here, that she had heard from anyone else in Hamilton recently?"

"Nope. Well—no."

"What, Jack?" prompted George. "It may be important."

"Important to who?" He glared at them and took a long pull at his bottle of beer. He had forsaken the beer mug as an unnecessary obstruction half an hour before.

"To all of us," said George patiently.

"To Jenny," added Dewey softly.

Riley looked at her carefully. Then he slowly loaded his fork and ate. Finally he spoke. "She said one thing. Maybe old mother Mildred might quit being so crazy, if she knew, or something. I thought it was nuts. Everybody knows Mildred Jones is around the bend."

"Knew what, Jack? Something about Tommy?"

Riley nodded. "She had good news for Tommy's mother, is what she said. I told her it was crazy. And look where it got her. Good news for Tommy's mother got my girl killed."

Jack Riley had departed, as full of good fellowship as he ever had been in twenty years. He had actually shaken Dewey's hand on the way out, which—George told her proudly as they washed the dishes—was a high compliment indeed from Jack Riley.

"Jack is such a sad creature," said Dewey. "I think he's convinced that the world has conspired against him."

George agreed. "Thinks he was born too late. Wants to be a frontiersman in the Old West."

Dewey shook his head. " 'The fault is not in our stars, but in ourselves, that we are underlings.' "

"Exactly right. But you did all right with him, my dear. He seemed to open up a bit."

But Dewey's mind was not on Jack Riley any longer.

"George, I have got to talk to Mildred Jones."

"About Jenny Riley? Whew—Dewey, you're a braver man than I am. That's all I can say."

"You do realize what this means, though, George?"

"Dewey, my sweet, don't leap to conclusions. We have no way of knowing what kind of news Jenny may or may not have had for Mildred."

"Do you think Mildred may have had something to do with all of this? Ooh, George. The look on her face that morning." She described the scene in the tent at the River Festival as Jenny Riley made her entrance.

"You know as well as I do, my dear, that Mildred Jones is liable to fits of ill temper."

"Yes. Yes, indeed."

"Promise me you'll tread carefully, Dewey." George dried his hands and settled them firmly on her shoulders. "Promise?"

"Yes, of course."

"Good. If there are clues to be had from Mildred Jones, you'll sniff them out. Eh, my sweet? Oh—speaking of clues. Bookie came by."

"Oh, dear. Is he very angry with me?" She briefly outlined her visit to the station this afternoon. "I was hoping that Sergeant Fenton might help me out, but we were caught in the act, I'm afraid."

George's eyes twinkled. "Contaminating the pipeline of authority, eh? You'd better watch your step, Dewey. As it happens, Bookie didn't mention your name once. Did decline my invitation to stay to supper. But you know, they found the poison bottle."

"Did they really? Where?"

"Josh Machen found it. He had the garbage detail. Right in one of the bags out back of the Hamilton Inn. Which reminds me. There was apparently a bit of a booby trap in Jenny Riley's room at the inn."

"You're joking!"

"No, sirree. Somebody had coated the bathtub in her room with butcher's wax."

"Good heavens." Dewey gazed thoughtfully at George. "She might have broken her neck."

George nodded. "The belt-and-suspenders approach, is what Bookie thinks. Ponseca was the only person who visited her room. If the poison misfired, well—"

"Oh, that's awful. Did Bookie find anything out about the poison?"

"Nothing new. It *was* nicotine sulfate, all right. Some garden thing, called 'Aphids Away.' But no prints, of course, and Bookie says they can't trace it around here. Rob Jensen says he didn't sell a bottle of it to anyone, although he carries that brand. And Abby Scott doesn't carry it."

"Oh, yes, I know. She recommends ladybugs." Dewey

smiled at George. "Well, George, you don't think I've been idle, do you?"

"Never, my dear. How about a nightcap?"

Dewey shook her head firmly. "George. We have to find out who wrote to Jenny Riley. I'm going home to think. 'The letter killeth,' you know."

20

"ISAIAH, I HAVE been thick as a brick about this whole thing," said Dewey James early the next morning. Isaiah wagged his tail, sat heavily on the floor, and regarded his mistress ponderously. She filled his bowl and placed it on the floor, gazing out through the kitchen window to the small pasture behind her house. Starbuck, her seedy and lovable chestnut mare, was chomping idly at the grass. "Decidedly thick, Isaiah. But we'll soon see to that, won't we? I have an idea, my friend." But Isaiah was no longer listening to her.

She looked at the clock. The school office would be open in another fifteen minutes. With luck she could collect her information in time to catch Fielding Booker on his way to the office, before the headaches of his day set in. She donned her purple cardigan and headed out for her car.

Isadora Hebb, the director of alumni affairs at Hamilton High, was a round, competent-looking woman of indeterminate age. Her graying hair was untidily gathered in a knot at the nape of her neck, as it had been since time immemorial. Isadora Hebb herself had been in this very spot since time immemorial. She was an energetic woman and remarkably good at her job. Hamilton High always had near-perfect attendance at the big reunions.

Isadora Hebb sorted through a stack of papers on her old-fashioned, heavy wooden desk, moving some to a pile in a corner, others to a row of rickety chicken-wire baskets on a lopsided bookcase. Hamilton High, home of the

126

Hornets (which every right-thinking American must acknowledge as the finest high school basketball team on earth) had its priorities. Working space for administrators was decidedly low on the list. But Isadora Hebb, like all good alumni of that august institution, found no fault with the order of things. She did her job uncomplainingly in the cramped, windowless box that passed for an office. She knew her place in a universe where all minor planets revolved around a basketball.

"Good morning, Isadora," said Dewey James tentatively. "Have I come at a bad moment?"

"Hello, Dewey." Isadora Hebb moved a pile of papers from one box to another. "I'm filing. My fail-safe system." She grinned. "What brings you here?"

"Goodness!" Dewey exclaimed, looking at the disaster area before her. "Won't they give you a filing cabinet?"

Isadora Hebb merely laughed. "Too late for that, I'm afraid. Wouldn't do any good at this point. That's all right—I happen to know where everything is."

"Yes, I'm sure you do. Makes you indispensable, anyway."

"Right." She looked inquiringly at Dewey.

"I wondered if I might ask you a question, Isadora."

"Anything. Only I'm afraid I can't offer you a seat." She smiled ruefully and gestured at her filing boxes, piled high on chairs. "All taken."

"That's quite all right. You see, the Homecoming Committee was just tidying up one or two things having to do with last weekend, and we've had a bit of a mix-up."

"Uh-huh. Are you sure this has to do with the Homecoming, Dewey?" Isadora Hebb regarded Dewey shrewdly.

"Well—yes. And no. That is—" She looked out into the long corridor behind her. It was empty, but just to be on the safe side, Dewey stepped firmly into the little room and closed the door.

"Goodness." Isadora Hebb's eyebrows shot up.

"This mustn't go beyond these four walls, Isadora," Dewey said sternly. "I'm afraid it's rather dangerous, my even being here."

"You want to ask me something about Jenny Riley."

"That's right. One question; and then please—forget that I was here. Will you do that for me?" Isadora Hebb nodded. Dewey knew that the woman could be trusted. "Good. It's this. Who called you, or wrote to you, or came by here, asking for Jenny's address?"

"How on earth do you know about that?" There was a pause as she surveyed her overflowing office. "I think we'd better clear off a seat for you," she said, making room for Dewey on a chair. "It's been bothering me, and I don't know why. Someone did call and ask me for her address. Said that she was calling for the Homecoming Committee." She shook her head. "I only thought of it again yesterday."

"When was this?"

"Oh—quite a long time ago. Two or three months, anyway. Just when things were starting up, I suppose, and you had begun to mail out all the letters to people."

"You said 'she.' Did your caller identify herself?"

She shook her head. "No. And you know, I thought it was funny at the time. Not funny, really. More—uncalled for. It irritated me that one of my friends in town could call me for information and not even have the time to say hello. But I didn't think about it again until just yesterday."

"You're certain it was a woman?"

"Yes. But I didn't recognize the voice."

"Well. Thank you very much, Isadora. And please," added Dewey as she prepared to leave, "don't mention this fact to anyone. I imagine it may be very important. But the last thing we want is for our poisoner to think that you are a threat to his—or her—imperfect peace of mind."

"Slow down, now, Dewey. Slow down, please, and tell me again what's bothering you." Fielding Booker was feeling more cheerful this morning. He had just had a report in from Baltimore, where something strange had turned up: It appeared that the name Alejandro Ponseca was known to city officials. He had scheduled a conference call with Baltimore's chief of detectives for 11:00 A.M.—in just two hours he would have his man. A gratified Fielding Booker was now prepared to meet the challenges of the day with good humor. He was back in the saddle again.

"Bookie, it's very simple," explained Dewey patiently. "As I said. When the Homecoming Committee sent out its invitations, we did not send one to Jenny Riley. But she got one—because she wrote us back to say that she would come."

Booker still wasn't certain what any of this had to do with Jenny's murder. "Dewey. You must have overlooked something."

Dewey James shook her head firmly. "Susan Miles was the committee secretary, and she has all the records."

"Well, then," said Booker amiably, "if you didn't send her an invitation, Dewey, how do you suppose she got one?"

"That's just it." Dewey related what she had discovered at the alumni office. "Don't you see, Bookie? The person who called Isadora Hebb could be our murderer."

Booker smiled and leaned forward, idly shaking the paper clip holder on his desk this way and that, watching the clips slide around inside. At last he spoke.

"Dewey, I'm going to talk to you in confidence. For two reasons. First," he held up a finger, "because I'm sure that I can trust you not to repeat confidential information. And second, because I think you have better things to do than to waste my time and your own chasing around after shadowy figures who write mysterious letters and make anonymous phone calls."

"But, Bookie—"

"Dewey, something big has come up in this business. Very big, indeed. I won't bore you with the details, but I will tell you that I am anticipating a telephone call in just a few hours that will wrap this thing up for us. Once and for all."

"Bookie, I don't think so." Dewey looked at him shrewdly. "I doubt you have a shred of evidence against that man. And I think you are embarked on a vendetta of a personal nature."

He looked at her sharply. "Has Fenton been talking to you about this case?"

"No, indeed, Bookie. But everyone in town knows that you have had Alejandro Ponseca in this office almost constantly. That you have searched his room at the inn and made many inquiries about his past. Tell me," she added, "am I wrong?"

Booker shook his head stubbornly. "Dewey, this is a small town, and it is my humble job to keep the peace. I will not allow the muscle of the rich people hereabouts to cloud my judgment on a case. And I refuse to be cowed by obscure threats and rumors about my own involvement," he added grandly. "Now. Suppose you do a little favor for me?"

"What's that, Bookie?"

"I'd like you to keep your own counsel on this whole affair."

"But, Bookie—"

"Sorry, Dewey. That's how it is." He smiled at her. "You know that I have the greatest respect for you."

"I know no such thing, Bookie. In fact, if pressed, I'd say that you think I'm a little bit off my rocker."

"No, Dewey, not at all. You are earnest and inquisitive. But this is a very serious police matter."

"I'm well aware of the seriousness of the matter, Bookie."

"Glad to hear it. Take my advice, Dewey. Please." There was real entreaty in his eyes. The last thing Fielding Booker wanted was Dewey's help and advice. She was extremely persuasive when she wanted to be; and Booker could ill afford the indulgent distractions of her theories.

Dewey knew she was not going to make Booker see the light—not just at present, anyway. Never mind. She had a fairly good idea who had written to Jenny Riley. Although getting Mildred Jones to admit it might take some work. It would be far easier, in a way, to pursue her ideas on her own. "I won't trespass further on your time, Bookie." She rose to her feet and collected her handbag and sweater.

Booker was suddenly alarmed. He knew that look of

acquiescence; it was a dangerous look. The last time he had seen it, Dewey James had come close to sinking a very complex investigation into the murder at Evergreen Farm. "Dewey. I want your promise."

"Bookie, honestly. I promise I won't bother you with idle speculation. There. Will that do?" She smiled brightly at him and departed.

21

ALL WAS NOT well at the In-Time School of Ballroom
Dance. Delphine Charlotte sensed as much the instant she
arrived at the studio at lunchtime on Wednesday. There was
something wrong in the air. With an unaccountable feeling
of dread, she pushed open the door to the small office and
looked about in alarm. The cramped and ill-furnished room
bore all the signs of a hasty and violent search. The two
drawers of the filing cabinet were half open, and papers
were scattered about.

"Damn!" she exclaimed. "Robbers." She looked about
the office. There was no sign of Norman Fox. "Norman?
You here?" she called out into the empty studio. She looked
at the clock on the wall. "Hey, Killer!" There was no reply.

Without knowing the reason for it, Delphine Charlotte
panicked. She ran, as fast as her supple legs would carry
her, downstairs and into the freshening April morning.

Sergeant Mike Fenton looked over the scene carefully. "Did
you touch anything, Miss Charlotte?"

Delphine shook her head.

"And you say you can't find your partner. Did you try his
home?"

"Yeah. I tried him from the filling station, right after I
called you. No answer."

"Was he supposed to be at the school today?"

She nodded. "For a noon lesson—our lunchtime special.
Except it doesn't look like anybody turned up."

"Is that where you keep your cash receipts?" Fenton gestured to a small steel strongbox on the desk.

Delphine shook her head again. "No. Money and checks in the safe—that little one, over there." She pointed toward a small, freestanding safe that stood open against the far wall. "But I took everything to the automatic teller last night, after I closed up."

"What time?"

"Nine, nine-fifteen. Around then."

"Where was Fox?"

"He was here. We left together. He said he was going home. I went to the bank, then home."

"What about this box, then?"

"That box is Norman's. He keeps private stuff in there— papers and stuff, I guess. I don't know about money."

Fenton leaned over and used a pencil to flip open the lid of the box. A small padlock on the front dangled futilely, its hasp wide open. The box was empty. "You sure about that?"

"Yeah, I'm sure. Except he usually keeps it at home. Don't know what it's doing here."

"All right, Miss Charlotte. You can go now. We'll have to dust for prints here. Can you find another spot to hold your classes today?"

"Don't have any classes." Delphine smiled. She gathered up her canvas bag and looked around with a sigh. "Looks like I don't have anything anymore." She left.

Fenton turned to Officer Kate Shoemaker, who was watching patiently from the doorway. "Kate, check the grounds. Out back. Everything. See if you can find something to indicate which way the burglars left here."

"Sir."

She departed, leaving Fenton to go to work on prints in the office. But within moments Kate Shoemaker reappeared in the doorway, her freckled face drawn and very pale.

"Mike, sir. Out back."

They descended and went down the narrow walkway to the alley behind the dance school.

The construction workers renovating the building next

door had hired a Dumpster for the discards of their labor. "In there." Officer Shoemaker pointed a finger, keeping steady with a will.

Fenton stepped up on a small ledge and peered over into the Dumpster. After a brief hesitation Kate Shoemaker followed suit. On the jagged pile of cinder blocks and lumber within, Norman Fox lay faceup, his legs and arms flailed awkwardly outward. His toupee had been caught on a protruding nail and sat up off his head like something alive; it seemed to regard them with the eyes of a curious, watchful rodent, jealous of its meal.

Fenton and Shoemaker stepped down.

"Radio the captain, Kate."

"He won't like this. I mean, didn't Mrs.—"

"That's right. You can do the honors." Fenton grinned at Officer Shoemaker. "You're going to be a great detective someday, Katie."

Fielding Booker came at once to the In-Time School of Ballroom Dance. Fenton and Shoemaker showed him their grisly discovery in the Dumpster out back; within a few minutes Robert Gaston, the county medical examiner, had duly arrived and pronounced Norman Fox dead.

"Cause of death, Doctor?"

Robert Gaston looked resignedly at Booker. "Captain. I will let you have the findings as soon as I can complete my postmortem."

"Off the record." Booker hated playing this game with Gaston. The medical examiner was always extremely cautious in making his determinations. But there was no way around it; Robert Gaston lived for the evidence of his laboratory.

"Off the record I'd say he died as a result of a blow to the skull. But I can't be certain until the tests are complete."

"Weapon? Time of death?"

Gaston breathed in and out heavily, then looked around at the construction site next door to the dance school. "Plenty of reinforced concrete bars handy. That might have done the trick. Time of death: I would be willing to hazard a guess

that the man has been dead between four and twenty hours."
He squatted down and lifted a corner of the blanket covering
the body. "Rigor is firmly established in the corpse. Of
course, you may be able to narrow that down some, with
other evidence."

"I should bloody well hope so," said Booker. "Fenton.
Where's that dancing woman?"

"Delphine Charlotte, sir. I sent her on home, before Kate
found him."

"Well. Kate, nice work. Suppose you go and pick her up.
Break the news to her and get her to headquarters, my girl.
On the double."

"Yessir."

The coroner's team took the body away, and Fielding
Booker returned upstairs to the studio with Fenton.

"You say she expected him to be here?" asked Booker as
he surveyed the office.

"She said there was some kind of class or something at
noon, sir."

"Hmmm." He squatted down and peered into the safe.
"How much money was taken?"

"None, sir. She had deposited all the cash and checks at
the bank last night. After she left here."

"What time was that?"

"Late. Nine o'clock or so. She used a machine."

"Check on that. I'm afraid you'll have to see Miss Mole
about it."

Fenton gave an involuntary shiver. Marjorie Mole, the
acting manager of the Warren State Savings and Loan, was
a particularly loathsome woman who sucked constantly on
foully sweet candies and was given to fits of giggles. "Yes,
sir."

"Or send Officer Machen. He's had it pretty easy the last
few days."

"Yes, sir." Fenton sounded relieved.

Booker looked at the metal strongbox on the desk. "What
did they keep in here?"

"Papers. Miss Charlotte says it was Fox's personal
stuff."

"Don't say 'stuff' to me, Fenton. You know better."

"Yes, sir. Personal items."

"Well, well. Looks like Mr. Fox turned up at the wrong moment. Caught them in the act, I bet you."

"Uh, sir, do you suppose that this incident is connected to the other murder?"

He looked at his sergeant. "Do you?"

"Well, sir, it's only that the other day, you may remember, that I mentioned to you how Mr. Fox was seen going, uh, upstairs at the Straw Hat Supper."

"Yes, so you did."

"Well, sir, don't you think that maybe he saw something?"

Booker sighed deeply. He didn't like the looks of this situation. "Tell me again, Mike, where you got that information."

"From Mrs. James, sir."

"Our ever-lovin' local librarian."

"Well, sir, Professor Renfrew—"

"Hah!" exclaimed Fielding Booker. "How do you explain, Mike, that of two hundred people present at the Straw Hat Supper, the only one who has come forward with that story is a lunatic who believes in human sacrifice?"

"Well, sir, there was a lot going on. Maybe nobody else was watching."

"They were watching, all right." Booker looked grim. "About a dozen of my neighbors are willing to swear they saw me carry a poisoned drink to that lovely girl. They were watching, Mike."

"Yes, sir."

Booker looked around the office once more. "I have a feeling about this whole thing. I will want to hear more about Mr. Norman Fox and his visit to the dressing room."

"If you'd like, sir, I can speak to Mrs. James again."

Booker heaved a huge sigh. "We'd better go and talk to her."

"Mrs. James, sir?"

"Mikey, Mikey. Lord, no. The dancing girl. Not Mrs. James. Anything but Dewey James."

They locked the door and departed.

* * *

When they arrived at police headquarters, Delphine Charlotte was waiting for them in Fielding Booker's office. She looked frightened.

"Miss Charlotte," said Booker, "I am very sorry about your partner."

"Thanks." Delphine Charlotte bit her lip. "He must have gone back for something."

"Tell me. What time, exactly, did you leave the dancing school?"

"About nine-fifteen, I think. Wait, I'll tell you." She rummaged in her pocketbook and drew out a handful of crumpled pieces of paper. "I have the deposit slip from the automatic teller. Here it is. Nine twenty-three."

Booker examined it and gave it back to her. "And Mr. Fox was going home, you say?"

"That's what he said."

"Miss Charlotte. Did Mr. Fox say anything to you about Alejandro Ponseca?"

"The dancer? No, I don't think Kill—Norman even knew him."

"But he knew all about him."

"Well, of course we talked about him. He's incredible."

"Exactly," replied Booker, nodding his head gently. "That's just the word I would use. Thank you, Miss Charlotte. That's all for now. We may need to see you again, however."

When she had gone, Booker turned to his sergeant. "Get that man in here. Right away."

"Yessir."

"Mr. Ponseca. You have just one more chance to tell me exactly where you were last night after nine-fifteen. Do I make myself clear?" Booker stopped his pacing and leaned heavily across the small metal table in the interrogation room. "Or would you like, sir, for me to arrange for a translator?"

Ponseca, sitting calmly at the table, shook his head. "There is no need for such a step, my dear captain. My

English is exceedingly good. As good as your own, in fact. Your diligent sergeant has no difficulty in taking down my every word." He looked benignly at Sergeant Fenton, who sat quietly in a chair in the corner, making notes of the interview.

"Well, if your problem is not linguistic, perhaps you are suffering from a deficiency of reason. Perhaps, sir, you would care to have your psychiatrist present. To make clear to you the lunacy of the course you are following."

"My good sir," replied Ponseca equably, "I assure you that I am not crazy. But if you refuse to do me the honor of explaining why you wish to pry into my private life, then I cannot extend to you the courtesy of an answer."

"You bloody fool!" shouted Booker, slamming a large hand down on the table. He pointed a finger at Ponseca. "I've got the goods on you, my man. The days of wine and roses are over. So talk to me, blast you."

Ponseca remained calm. "What sort of 'goods' can you possibly mean, Captain? My life is an open book." He gestured widely with his hands, his smile open and relaxed.

"Yes, indeed," said Booker, chuckling. "It most certainly is—now. I have been in touch with the authorities in Baltimore." Booker watched in satisfaction as Ponseca dropped his hands to his sides, paling visibly. The dancer's smile remained fixed, but it had lost its punch. Booker went on. "And tomorrow morning I will have on my desk a full report of your past."

With an effort Ponseca returned to his easy manner. He regarded the back of one hand and spoke at last. "I cannot imagine what concern you have with the little doings of my life, Captain. I thought it was your job to investigate the murder of my friend and partner."

"Oh, is that what you thought, eh?" Booker chuckled and pulled a chair around. He sat, heavily complacent. "Mr. Ponseca," he said in tones of soft, reasoning persuasion, "perhaps you will feel more inclined to cooperate with me if I tell you that further violence has been done in this town."

"But—of what kind? You must tell me."

"Certainly, if you like. A Mr. Norman Fox was found murdered, sir. My officers found his body this noontime."

"I am sorry, Captain. The name means nothing to me."

"Well, now, we shall see about that. As it happens, the police were on the point of questioning Mr. Fox. We have witnesses who confirm that Norman Fox paid a visit to the gallery shortly before your performance began. When you and the unfortunate Miss Riley were alone on the second floor, preparing to go on stage."

If Sergeant Fenton was surprised at this assertion, he was far too well trained to show it. He only wished that the captain had acted sooner on Dewey James's tip. Whatever Norman Fox had seen, it was too late to get it out of him.

"Now," pursued Booker, glowering at the dancer. "Suppose you tell me what you were up to last night, eh?"

But Ponseca remained stubbornly silent. "I am sorry, sir. But my honor as a gentleman is not such a trifle that I could toss it away, like that"—he snapped his fingers—"at the mere say-so of the police. No matter how much I may esteem you for your intelligence and your good taste." He shook his head and glanced at his watch. "If you will excuse me, I have an appointment."

"Like hell you do." Booker rose and turned to his sergeant. "Fenton."

"Sir."

"Mr. Ponseca will be remaining here as our guest. If you will be so kind as to make the necessary arrangements." He fixed his glance on Ponseca. "And bear in mind, Mikey, that our guest is every inch a gentleman."

"Yessir." Sergeant Fenton closed his notebook and stood.

Ponseca at last began to look sincerely troubled. "Captain Booker, I demand to know what right you have to hold me here."

"I'm holding you for questioning, sir, in connection with two homicides. In this country, you know, we frown on murder. Even when it is done for the sake of honor."

22

THE LITTLE TOWN of Hamilton was shaken by the news of Norman Fox's sudden departure from this life. Not that anyone in town particularly minded his going. Even the well-intentioned Delphine couldn't mourn for her partner.

No, it was not his going, but the way in which he had gone, that upset Hamiltonians. Before suppertime on Wednesday evening, tongues had begun to wag. Was it true that Norman Fox had seen Fielding Booker in Jenny's dressing room? Yes, said those who felt it must be so. Was it true that Alejandro Ponseca had killed a rival dancer in retribution for the death of Jenny Riley? Naturally. It was the kind of thing a real man did, to avenge the woman he loved.

Love had nothing to do with it, sneered Ponseca's detractors. The killing had been carried out in classic execution style. Alejandro Ponseca was a drug runner; someone knew for certain that Norman Fox had been found blindfolded, with his shoes on the wrong feet. Every schoolchild knew that was how they did things in Brazil.

Ponseca's partisans, however, scoffed at the notion. It was clear that Fox had been silenced by the police, who were already so deeply involved that they had been forced to kill again. It was all a clumsy attempt at a cover-up. There should be a special prosecutor appointed by the FBI to expose the forces of corruption in their town.

In her pink-toned, deeply cushioned apartment on the edge of town, Mary Barstow examined her face in the bathroom mirror and brooded. Perhaps she ought to give Captain Booker a call. He must be feeling lonely, with all the town suspecting him of two murders.

Doris Bock, on the other hand, was feeling anything but lonely. She had been obliged to keep the Tidal Wave open an hour later than usual, owing to the heavy flow of customers.

In the offices of the *Quill* Mary and Sonny Royce quickly remade the front page for this week's edition, congratulating themselves, as they scanned in a photo of Norman Fox, on the purchase of their powerful new computer.

Over a solitary whiskey (neat) in the lounge at the Hamilton Inn, Professor Renfrew nodded silently to himself and made a note in his diary. This would make a persuasive footnote to his lecture tomorrow up at Farrand State University.

At Leithdown Farm Henrietta Ambler had placed a call to Senator Davidson and then taken to her bed with a headache. The impenetrable Brant, sensing his mistress's unhappiness, answered the telephone with unusual alacrity and explained to callers in a soft voice that Madam was unwell. He allowed them to infer what they might from this fact.

At home, feeding her horse and her dog, Dewey James thought. George Farnham had called her with details of Kate Shoemaker's gruesome discovery in the Dumpster; the news hadn't really surprised her. As she gave Starbuck a good brushing, Dewey recalled the small portion of Fox's telephone conversation, which she had overheard the day before. What had he said? Something about a rendezvous at eleven o'clock. Had that been an appointment for the morning or for the night? Dewey stroked the mare's nose thoughtfully.

"What do you make of it, old girl?" she asked. The mare nudged at the pocket of Dewey's sweater. "Yes, my lovely creature." Dewey reached into the pocket and withdrew an apple for Starbuck. "You work on this," she said, holding the apple out on her palm. "And I'll go to work on that woman."

Delphine Charlotte lived in a small, dark apartment in the old mill district, not far from George Farnham's house.

Dewey had telephoned to say she would like to come by for a short visit; Delphine had been surprised at Dewey's call but willing enough to talk.

Now they were seated in Delphine's living room. Dewey was perched upright on a small wooden armchair. Delphine sat with her legs tucked under her on a worn but comfortable-looking sofa; a large gray cat had made himself at home in her lap. There was another cat curled up asleep beside her. Delphine had made no pretense of grieving for Norman Fox, but she was still evidently shocked.

"I always thought Norman would make enemies. I didn't think he'd get himself killed. But he was a pretty shady guy, Mrs. James."

"I—er—had surmised as much, you know. I talked to him about lessons, and he gave me a very curious contract to sign."

"Oh." Delphine looked uncomfortable. "You don't have to worry about that," she said generously. "I won't hold you to it."

Dewey smiled. "Never fear, Miss Charlotte. I didn't sign it."

Delphine was relieved. "Good. Hey, Mrs. James. I been wondering all day. You think Norm getting killed might have something to do with Jenny Riley?"

Dewey vigorously nodded. "I do indeed." She briefly outlined what Professor Renfrew had seen on the night of Jenny's murder. "It was after you and Mr. Fox had left the dance floor. I thought you had both gone, but apparently Mr. Fox stayed on for the festivities."

"Yeah. So you think maybe he saw the murderer?"

"Yes—or something to indicate who the murderer was. Don't you?" Dewey raised a quizzical brow. Delphine shrugged and pushed the cat aside. "Miss Charlotte—"

"Please call me Delphine."

"All right, I will. If you'll call me Dewey."

"Okay, Dewey." Delphine smiled, and her deep brown eyes lit up. It struck Dewey that this woman was lonely; there were, heaven knew, few clients at the In-Time School of Ballroom Dance. But Delphine seemed to bear her loneliness well. The apartment, although dark and small, had been tastefully furnished with inexpensive second-hand items. There was a fancy-looking record player in one corner and a large bookcase along a wall, holding volumes that were obviously well thumbed. The cats were rather dubious; but that was the nature of cats. Dewey must remember, when all this was through, to see if Delphine would care to join the library's Literacy Volunteers.

"Delphine—if you'll forgive the meddling intrusions of an old lady—what were you and Norman Fox arguing about that evening?"

Delphine laughed. "Norman was just being himself. It was enough to make me mad."

"I see. But you seemed to be having a rather intense conversation during the cha-cha. May I ask what you talked about?"

"Oh, nothing, really. Norm was always on to something big. At least, that's the way he talked. He was telling me he had the goods on somebody in town and was going to make him pay through the nose."

"Good heavens! You mean blackmail?"

Delphine nodded. "I figured it was just talk. He was like that. We were dancing, talking about everybody. You know." She looked momentarily abashed, but Dewey smiled on her kindly.

"Yes, I do know. George Farnham and I were engaged in the same sport."

"Yeah. Well, so he says, looking over toward where Jenny was sitting, that he had a nasty little surprise up his sleeve for somebody."

"For Jenny?"

Delphine shook her head. "Nope, that was what I thought at first. But when I mentioned her name, he just told me to shut up. But he was watching somebody, across the room."

"You don't know who?"

"Nah. I was facing the other way."

"Yes, I see. Go on."

"So I asked him what he was talking about, and he said,

'I'm looking at my ticket outta this dump, toots.' Or something like that."

"Did you have any idea what he meant?"

Delphine shook her head. "He was always saying stuff like that. Thought he was a gangster or something."

"I see. Did you find him a good business partner? Trustworthy, and so forth?"

"I didn't have much choice. But he wasn't a very nice guy. And I think he'd been in some kind of trouble in New York. That's why he came out here, to a little town where nobody knew him."

"Yes. I rather wondered why Mr. Fox had determined to grace Hamilton with his presence. Well. You say he claimed to 'have the goods' on someone. Was this what made you angry with him?" she asked, recalling the vicious slap Delphine had administered that evening.

"Oh—no. No—he just got crude on me. He was always saying things that got under my skin, like. But he—well, he said something worse than usual. And I decided I'd had enough. So I let him have it."

"I see." Dewey grew thoughtful. One of Delphine's cats began to rub himself against her ankles, and the dancer reached down absentmindedly to stroke it. "Delphine, I went to see Mr. Fox on the—er, the pretense of wishing to sign up for dancing lessons. But I'm afraid I wasn't altogether honest with him yesterday morning. I was curious, you see, because of what I had learned from Professor Renfrew." Dewey thought again about the way that Fox had steered clear of Jenny Riley's table. "And because of something else which I witnessed on Saturday night. It made me wonder if there was some connection between Mr. Fox and Jenny Riley. I don't suppose he talked to you about her?"

Delphine looked at Dewey with rising interest. "You know, I *thought* there was something weird about him and her. I mean, he always acted kinda strange when her name came up. But when I asked him about it, he told me to shut up."

"Mr. Fox seems to have been rather fond of telling you to

shut up," Dewey remarked. "Did you think that he was hiding something?"

"Kind of. But nothing obvious. Norm liked to think he was real tricky. He said he didn't know her from New York, but I got the feeling maybe he knew something about her."

"I see." Dewey pondered. "About her connection to people here?"

"Yeah."

Whatever it was that Fox had known about Jenny Riley, it must have had to do with her life in New York, Dewey reasoned. The girl had not been home in twelve years. And somehow, in New York, the connection to Hamilton had been made. Dewey sat up with a start.

"What? Did you think of something, Dewey?"

"Yes, Delphine. I rather imagine I have thought of something."

As she headed for her car, Dewey thought long and hard about the business. There was only one way that everything seemed to make sense to her. She reviewed the facts in her mind carefully, point by point, filing them away on little mental index cards.

Delphine had thought Norman Fox's plans to blackmail someone were all talk. But his subsequent murder led Dewey to believe that he had indeed intended to get his "ticket outta this dump"; and who made for a more promising blackmail victim than the very rich? She would turn her attention to that question tomorrow morning. There was one more little visit she planned to make this evening.

23

MOST OF THE Homecoming guests had departed (in one way or another, reflected Dewey grimly), and the Hamilton Inn had been restored to its customary level of genteel repose. Dewey entered the cool shadows of the sleepy lobby and looked about for Mildred Jones. She was there, behind the reception desk, doing the *Quill* acrostic. Dewey summoned her courage and marched to the desk.

"Hello, Mildred."

Mildred Jones looked up from her puzzle. "Afternoon, Mrs. James. If you've come to see your friend, he's not here." She smiled. "He's just down the street. A guest of the town."

"Oh. No—actually, I didn't come to see Mr. Ponseca, Mildred. But I did wonder if I might be able to talk to you for a moment or two."

"To me?" Mildred Jones muttered something under her breath and looked unhappily at Dewey James. "About what?"

"Well—about Jenny Riley."

"I don't have anything to say about that girl. I told you already, Mrs. James, I'm sorry she got herself killed like she did. There's nothing else to say."

"Oh, but I think there is, Mildred. And I think, you know, that you may be able to help find the person who did it. If I could just put one or two questions your way."

"Not me, Mrs. James. I don't know anything about it."

"Well—you see, I have an idea, Mildred, that you may know something, without knowing that you know. If you follow me." Dewey looked firmly at Mildred Jones, who shrugged.

"Ask away," she replied ungraciously.

"Thank you. I guess you've heard about the second murder in town—Norman Fox." Mildred Jones nodded. "I think that man must have seen something the night of the Homecoming. And I hoped you might be able to tell me if Jenny and Tommy had known him in New York."

"I don't know anything about that."

"Tommy didn't write to you about Norman Fox? Or mention his name in any way?"

"No. He knows I don't want anything to do with Jenny Riley's dancing friends. If they were *friends*." Her voice was heavy with irony. She looked at her watch. "I have to get back to work, Mrs. James."

"Yes, yes. Of course you do, Mildred, and I won't keep you more than one minute longer. It's very good of you to talk to me at all."

"What is it?"

"I spoke to Jack Riley the other day. He was terribly upset, naturally. But he mentioned something about Jenny having some kind of news for you. Do you know what he was talking about?"

"She was lying. She was full of it, that girl."

"Had she communicated with you, Mildred?"

Mildred Jones nodded. "I saw her down at the tent that day. I didn't want to speak to her, but she was pushy. All full of phony baloney about how much she cared about Tommy, and how he was getting much better, and soon he would be out of—of that place."

"What made her think so?"

"I don't know, Mrs. James. But she was lying to me anyway. There's nothing good for Tommy."

"Oh, I wouldn't say that, Mildred. Tommy is a very bright and capable young man. I'm certain he will pull himself together." She looked carefully at Mildred Jones. "And at least Tommy still has his life before him. But she didn't tell you about anything specific? Something exciting, Jack seemed to think."

Mildred Jones seemed to come to a decision. She reached for her handbag and opened it slowly, keeping a wary eye on Dewey as she did so. She retrieved a letter and held it out to Dewey. "Read this."

Dewey opened the envelope. It was a letter from Tommy to his mother, written in a shaky but determined hand and dated last week.

Dear Mom,

Thanks for the letter and the socks. (Argyles! I'm a fashion plate!) I think I'll have to get myself a spiffy new pair of loafers, maybe some knickerbockers, to show them off in, as soon as I get out of here. What would you say to Bermuda shorts? They're all the rage.

I wish you would stop worrying about me. Everything is going to be just fine. I saw Jenny the other day. She seemed excited about the big Homecoming deal. (Please be nice to her, Mom, when you see her.) I guess it's no surprise I didn't get invited, considering everything. But one of these days I'll be at the top of the guest list—just you watch.

Anyway. Listen—I have a surprise for you. I'm not going to tell you what it is until I'm sure it's all set. But before long I'll be your famous—no longer infamous—blue-eyed boy. And it's something I couldn't have done before; so even you, Ma, will have to find the silver lining in my little cloud.

Hope the big Homecoming is fun. Haven't seen Jenny and Alejandro strut their stuff (we don't get much in the way of road trips, out here in the loony-boonies), but I hear she's terrific. I think even you will like it, Ma.

Gotta go. Big game of bridge in the rec. room, and we all take turns being dummy, which makes for a change. My friend Kevin says we ought to be able to play two-handed, but I told him that was a joke in poor taste. I'll write again soon.

Love,
Tommy

The letter made Dewey sad. She saw in it the high-spirited and intelligent boy that Tommy Jones had been, before the world had crashed around him. She handed it back to his mother. "He sounds cheerful enough, Mildred. I think that's a very good sign."

"Sign of what?"

"Well—that he's at least facing up to his situation."

"She did it to him," said Mildred Jones venomously. "He was crazy for her. See how crazy?" She shook the letter in Dewey's face, her dark eyes glittering. "And then as soon as Tommy got sick, she left him for that Spaniard."

"I don't think so, Mildred. I would guess that Jenny was a real friend to Tommy through his difficulties. You can see that she went to visit him and kept him up on things. And he's so proud of her." Dewey shook her head sadly. "Has he heard the news?"

"No. At least, not from me. I just couldn't." Mildred Jones began to cry, very softly. She looked away. "If you'll excuse me, Mrs. James. There's work to be done here."

Dewey, feeling angry and impotent, departed.

Whatever Jenny's news had been, Dewey was sure it was the same as Tommy's "surprise" for his mother. There was one simple way to find out—to write to Tommy and ask him. But Dewey shrank from the idea. If Mildred Jones was correct, Tommy probably had not even yet heard the news of Jenny's death. And Dewey knew very little of the medical realities of Tommy's situation. Perhaps Mildred would communicate with his doctor, or some kind of social worker at the hospital, to have them break the news. Or perhaps, one day next week, Dewey would herself get on a plane to New York and drive upstate along the Hudson River to Tommy's hospital. Tommy needed a friend. And if Mildred Jones had sent that Homecoming invitation to Jenny Riley, Dewey couldn't bear to think of it. She was glad to give that aspect of the whole thing a rest. She hated to think what might happen to Tommy if he learned the truth about that.

For tonight, Dewey James was tired. Her dealings with Mildred Jones had left a bad taste in her mouth. Dewey felt suddenly very sorry for the ignorant and mean-spirited woman. She reflected, as she drove home through the gathering darkness, that Mildred Jones and Jack Riley had much in common. They were both singularly ill-equipped to nurture the bright and shining lights, now dimmed, that they had brought into the world.

24

EARLY THE NEXT morning Dewey James climbed in her car and headed once more for Leithdown Farm. As the sun began a gentle ascent in the sky, she reflected that Henrietta Ambler was probably still asleep. No matter. She would see Dewey.

Brant opened the door and regarded Dewey impassively. "Yes, madam?"

"Good morning, Brant. Could you please tell Mrs. Ambler that I'm here? I won't keep her a minute, but it's vital that I talk to her."

"Very good, madam." Brant allowed Dewey to pass and left her once more to wait beneath the strikingly soulless painting in the front hall. Dewey felt certain it had cost a good deal of money; she was glad she didn't have to live with such an abomination.

Brant returned on silent feet. "Mrs. Ambler will see you upstairs, if you care to follow me." He led the way up a grand, sweeping staircase that didn't begin to fit the proportions of the hallway. It was so simple to ruin a house if you gave your pretensions full rein, thought Dewey.

Henrietta Ambler, wrapped sleekly in a mauve dressing gown with gold trim, sat on a white loveseat in a room that could only be called a boudoir. There was a small white desk in one corner and a dressing table in the other. Lacy white and pink curtains framed the large bay window, which gave out onto the rolling pastures on this side of the paddocks. The carpet under Dewey's feet was thick and soft.

"Dewey, dear. I won't get up, and you must forgive my appearance. I've had an absolutely shattering headache for the last twenty-four hours." Dewey could believe it. Henrietta Ambler's face was a mask of exhaustion and pain.

"Hello, Henrietta," she replied.

"What brings you here this morning? Here, sit down, darling." She patted the air in the direction of an overstuffed armchair, and Dewey took a seat. "Do you want that man to bring you something? Coffee, or tea?"

"No, thank you. I'm sorry you're feeling poorly, Henrietta, and I won't keep you a minute. But you see, I thought that you might want to talk to someone. So I came."

"Ahhh. You've worked it out, I see." She breathed in deeply. "One does such strange things, Dewey. And then wonders why, on earth, did I do that?"

"Well, Henrietta, I wouldn't call it strange. Unexpected, perhaps. But completely understandable."

"Oh! Do you think so?"

"Of course. Mr. Ponseca is a thoroughly charming man."

"As all successful cads must be, I suppose, if they are to get anywhere in this life. Ah, well. Time wounds all heels."

"Do you think he's a cad, Henrietta?" Dewey was surprised. "I rather like him."

"Do you really? I mean, you really do? But, Dewey, it's all over town that he's been arrested for that poor girl's murder! But I don't believe he did it!"

"I'm afraid Captain Booker has lit upon the wrong man. And I'm afraid, too, Henrietta, that you are partly to blame."

"Yes, I suppose I am. I rather got his goat, didn't I? But it all seemed so obvious. Fielding Booker is *such* a hopeless sleuth, you know, but I couldn't think of a good reason why he mightn't make a perfectly respectable murderer."

"You owe him an apology."

"I suppose I do." She grew thoughtful. "Do you really like Alejandro, Dewey?"

"Oh, yes. Quite a lot. That is—he's not quite the genuine article, you know."

"Oh, yes, I know. That was easy enough to see, the

moment he arrived here. You should have seen the way he looked at Brant. Not used to being buttled."

"Not many of us are, these days," replied Dewey with a laugh.

"But at least," Henrietta Ambler went on, "he had the decency not to tell me he was secretly a member of the Argentine royal family or any nonsense like that. I suppose he is rather a good sort, in his way."

"Just so. Henrietta." Dewey looked at the wealthy widow steadily. "I take it you have heard all about Norman Fox?"

"Oh, yes. That dreadful man with the lemur for a wig. Brant came to me with the news, yesterday afternoon. Odd, isn't it? We're having a crime wave in Hamilton. But then, you know all about crime, Dewey."

"Henrietta—it appears to me that the person who killed Norman Fox is also Jenny Riley's killer."

"No, *seriously*, Dewey?" Henrietta Ambler's face brightened. "Well, then, that means that Alejandro . . ."

"Yes?"

"Well, you see, he was here night before last. With me."

"I thought perhaps that might be the case. He refused, you know, to tell Booker where he was."

"Did he really?" She sat up and smiled. "Isn't that the nicest thing you've ever heard, Dewey? Who says chivalry is dead? You're a dear, an absolute dear, to come and tell me all this marvelous news. I owe you something in exchange."

Dewey was beginning to feel that Henrietta Ambler's troubles were not yet nearing their end, however. "Henrietta—did you ever meet Norman Fox?"

"What?" She laughed. "Meet that man? No, Dewey, I don't think so. Why ever do you ask?"

"Because I think he was trying to extort money from someone in town. And it did occur to me, you know, that a person given to such a crude activity would be most likely to choose a victim with deep pockets."

"Yes, I suppose so. I don't think there's much in my life that would be suitable blackmail material, Dewey. Even if there were, I should hardly give in to a little nobody like that."

"No, I didn't suppose you would." Dewey rose to go. "I hope we'll see you at the library tomorrow, Henrietta. Five o'clock."

"The library?"

"Alfred's party, in honor of his book. You are coming, aren't you?"

Henrietta waved a hand vaguely. "I suppose I really must turn up. What are you serving, Dewey? Not that dreadful sherry of yours."

Dewey smiled. "I'll let you have the vermouth."

"I don't know why Abby married that man. I can't stand him—an absolute newt for backbone. Worthless. The only thing he's ever done, that I can see, is write that silly book of his. I shouldn't wonder if he had help with the whole thing, from start to finish. Very well, then." Henrietta Ambler waved Dewey away. "I shall come. After all, he is family."

Dewey, suppressing a smile, took her leave.

25

"I PROMISE YOU, Bookie, I don't meant to interfere. But there are a few things you really ought to know. I would be remiss if I didn't tell you."

Fielding Booker smiled. For once he had beaten Dewey James to the punch. As he had remarked to Sergeant Fenton only last night, there was no substitute for hard work—especially good, old-fashioned police work, carried out by a team of sharp professionals. But he was willing to let Dewey talk. It would be the only way, he knew, to keep her from coming back to see him over and over and over again.

"Well, now, Dewey. I wouldn't want to get between you and a clear conscience. So you go right ahead and tell me whatever it is you need to. Get it off your chest, so to speak."

"Good. Well, first of all—I hate to say it, Bookie, but you've arrested the wrong man."

"Oho! Is that right? What makes you think so?"

"Bookie, I'm convinced that there is a murderer loose in Hamilton at present."

"Not loose, Dewey," he corrected her gently, with a nod toward the back of the building. "All safely tucked away."

"Oh, dear. No. Bookie—I am here to tell you, first of all, that Mr. Ponseca was not—er, alone, on the night that Norman Fox was murdered." She turned slightly pink.

Booker swallowed, looked hard at Dewey, and then laughed. "I don't believe it, Dewey. That man has stood the women in town on their heads." He leaned forward and spoke softly. "Ponseca says he's too much of a gentleman to

155

confess his whereabouts. I'd have thought, well, all things considered, Dewey—" He broke off, reddening. "That is to say—"

"Oh, good heavens, Bookie!" Dewey laughed. "It's not *my* reputation that Mr. Ponseca was seeking to safeguard."

"It's not?" Booker was relieved. He preferred to keep intact his mythologized image of the widow of Captain Brendan James.

"Although," Dewey added with a mischievous grin, "he most certainly has a way with him. I hate to think what might happen if I gave him the slightest encouragement."

"Well. I am glad to hear that, Dewey." He looked at her carefully. "Then how is it that you know he has an alibi?"

"I have it on the best authority. Really. Bookie—have you ever known Henrietta Ambler to take to her bed with a sick headache?" Booker shook his head. "It's positively Victorian, or possibly Edwardian. Makes you think of Disraeli, and Edward the Eighth, and the Free Love Movement. But that's all beside the point. I saw her this morning."

Booker was suddenly troubled. With this one piece of information Dewey had shattered his equanimity. There was still a chance, of course, that she was wrong. But through Fielding Booker's mind there flashed the memories of those other occasions on which he had fervently hoped that Dewey James was wrong. Her average, unfortunately for Booker, was distressingly good.

"Now, Dewey. I'm not saying that you're right about that fellow's alibi. You know what women will say, when they think they're helping a fellow that they, er, care for. But, for the sake of argument, let's suppose you are correct. You still can't get around the fact that he is the only one with motive, means, and opportunity."

"Well, honestly, Bookie. You might at least include yourself."

Her thrust went home. Booker looked truly shocked. "You don't seriously mean that, Dewey."

"Of course not. But, Bookie—where is there the slightest shred of proof that Alejandro Ponseca handled the poison?"

"We found it in the trash at the Hamilton Inn."

"Anyone could have put it there."

Booker shook his head firmly. "Sorry, Dewey. That won't work. We had that place carefully watched."

"We'll settle this point later, Bookie. For now, please, concentrate on a few things that have crept into my mind like a fog. 'On little cat feet.' If you grant him an alibi for Tuesday night, Bookie, you have got to admit it puts Ponseca more or less out of the running. Am I right? Or do you perhaps believe that the two murders are unrelated?"

Booker sighed. He was up a creek, and he knew it. But Fielding Booker's motto was "When you're up a creek, paddle like mad." He stirred uneasily in his chair. "Maybe they are. Dewey, we still haven't even found the weapon that was used to kill Norman Fox. We can't be absolutely certain that the two crimes are linked," he offered, faltering.

"Bookie. You could at least have the grace to blush when you offer me such fatuity in place of logic. We both know that you don't for one minute believe that."

"You're right, Dewey," he replied heavily. "I don't. But I'm sure he's our man."

"You're not sure of any such thing. You just want him to be. Your reasons are your own," she added gently. Dewey hadn't forgotten the look of pride on Booker's face as he carried Jenny Riley's drink upstairs to the gallery. "What we must do now is to put our heads together. And I would like to give you some rather interesting information."

"So you said, Dewey, about an hour ago. All right. Let's hear it."

"Bookie, I think Norman Fox was killed because he was blackmailing someone. And, unfortunately for him, that someone turned his hand to murder. Norman Fox tried to—what is the term?—'shake him down' for more money. And so, unfortunately, he was killed."

"Whoa, now, wait a minute. Dewey—I have heard you invent some pretty fancy things in my day, but this beats all. Whatever put blackmail into your head?"

"I had a long, cozy chat with Delphine yesterday

afternoon. It seems that Mr. Fox had made mention to her of some little scheme to purchase what he referred to as his 'ticket outta this dump.' Such an unfortunate way to describe our pretty little town, don't you think?"

"Yes, yes." Booker was impatient. He picked up a pencil and began to doodle on the blotter. "We have no proof of that, Dewey."

"We haven't looked for it. I think you should begin with a search, a very careful search, of his residence. I imagine that we are looking for some kind of correspondence, but I can't be certain until I see it. If you like, I'll help with the searching."

Booker was appalled at the notion, but he contained himself. "Thank you, Dewey," he remarked politely, "but that won't be necessary. I rather think my staff can handle that little job. Machen!"

Officer Josh Machen appeared in the doorway to Fielding Booker's office.

"Yes, sir."

"I want you to go over Fox's place with a fine-tooth comb. On the double. And take Kate with you."

"Yessir. What are we looking for, sir?"

Booker looked enquiringly at Dewey. "Perhaps you'd better ask the expert."

"Oh, dear heavens. I'm not certain, Officer Machen. But I think what you might look for is some kind of notebook or diary, in which Mr. Fox may have made notations. Or a pocket calendar."

"To show his appointments and stuff, you mean? His customers in Hamilton?"

"Oh, no. Goodness—sorry, Officer Machen. No, we're looking for last year's calendar. When Mr. Fox still lived in New York."

"Gotcha." He departed. Booker looked at Dewey.

"Satisfied?"

"My, yes. That was quick work. I also think, Bookie, that you will probably find that Mr. Fox has some sort of criminal record. I had the impression that he is no stranger to courts and police and judges."

"Oh, damn. I should have told Machen to lift some prints. Machen!"

Sergeant Fenton appeared in the doorway in answer to Booker's summons. "Gone, sir."

"Oh—here," said Dewey, rummaging in her handbag. "I think this should do the trick." She pulled out an envelope and handed it to Sergeant Fenton. "You'll find all the prints you need right there, Sergeant Fenton."

Fenton took the envelope, then looked warily from Dewey to Booker. He was beginning to understand how Fielding Booker felt about Dewey James and her helpful hints.

"Uh—check your envelope for prints, Mrs. James?" the sergeant asked politely.

"Heavens, no, Mike. I may be an amateur, but I hope I've watched enough episodes of *Perry Mason* to know a few things about murders. No—inside. Careful," she added.

Fenton cautiously extracted the paper within. It was Dewey's contract with the In-Time School of Ballroom Dance. "I don't get it, Mrs. James. What's this got to do with Jenny Riley?"

"Fox's fingerprints, man," said Booker impatiently. "Get them on the wire to New York City, pronto."

Mike Fenton scratched his head. Maybe the old man was losing his mind, right before his very eyes. "Yessir." He turned to Dewey. "Uh, Mrs. James—won't *your* fingerprints be on this?"

She shook her head. "Not on the front. I was *very* careful about that."

Booker rose and walked with Dewey to the front door. He wouldn't be happy again, he knew, until she was gone. No matter how right or wrong her little ideas might prove.

Suddenly the telephone rang on the front desk.

"Hamilton Police, Sergeant Fenton." Mike Fenton listened for a moment. Then he covered the phone. "Uh, sir—it's that call you've been expecting from Baltimore."

Booker looked up. He had momentarily forgotten about

his inquiries into Ponseca's shady past. Was there a hope, a faint chance, that he had been right all along?

He looked at Dewey, who smiled at him meekly. "Go on, Bookie. Take your call. I'm on my way, I promise."

"Thank you, Dewey." Booker grasped the phone from Fenton and spoke. "Captain Fielding Booker here. Yes, yes, thank you for getting back to us." He looked up at Dewey, who seemed to be taking her time getting through the door. He gave her a very dark look. Correctly interpreting its import, she went on out into the spring air.

26

THE LITTLE TOWN of Hamilton had never known such excitement in a single week. Two murders, a Homecoming, and now, on Thursday afternoon, the sherry party at the library to celebrate the publication of Alfred Scott's first novel. Had they been formed of less hardy stock, Hamiltonians might have found the times exhausting. But Hamiltonians are sturdy, and rise to every occasion, no matter how tiring or extreme.

Dewey was pleased with the turnout at the library. They had at least fifty people there, she reckoned—and, as an added bonus, Professor Renfrew had departed. Tom Campbell tut-tutted. He had even gone so far as to suggest that the sherry party ought to be rescheduled to accommodate the learned ghoul's schedule; but Dewey had put her foot down.

Alfred Scott was in fine form. Dewey had stationed him in the reference section, and on the table before him were several copies of *Blues*. He bore his celebrity with meek pride, smiling on his public and trying, from time to time, to amuse them all with deft little jests befitting an author. From her station at the circulation desk, Dewey could see Mary Barstow grinning up at Alfred with a wide-eyed and adoring smile. For Hamilton men there was no curse quite like the interest of Mary Barstow. Dewey felt sorry for Alfred.

"Well, my dear," said George Farnham to Dewey, refilling his glass at the circulation desk. "I think you ought to consider another line of work."

"George, what on earth are you talking about?" Dewey smiled at him.

"Look around. Second big wingding in this place in a week. Lots of money in throwing parties, Dewey. Festivities consulting. You know. Like those ladies who write books about which gingham place mats go best with blueberry pie."

"Ah, yes. Except you'll notice, George, that there is neither gingham nor pie in the library today."

"Easily remedied, my dear. You even got the constabulary to turn out for this one, I see." He nodded toward Fielding Booker, deep in consultation with Sonny Royce in the children's section.

Dewey shook her head. "Poor Bookie. He hates being grilled by the press—such as it is. He had to let Alejandro Ponseca go, you know."

"So I heard," replied George with a heartfelt chuckle. "Little case of *noblesse oblige,* would you say, Dewey?"

Dewey laughed. "More like *droit de maîtresse.*" She looked toward Booker. Sonny Royce was now taking notes. "I wonder what on earth he will do about this mess, George."

"He ought to put you to work on it, my dear."

"Well—he was rather good about listening to one or two small suggestions that I had for him yesterday." She briefly described her visit to the police station and her conviction that Norman Fox was attempting to blackmail someone in town. "But I don't see how he'll ever get to the bottom of it, George. I saw Mike Fenton this morning, and he says that a thorough search of Norman Fox's belongings turned up nothing. Absolutely nothing."

Tom Campbell called for attention and prevailed upon a becomingly reluctant Alfred Scott to make a small speech. Everyone listened politely, if without interest, to Alfred's rambling monologue, in which he compared, with an astonishing lack of originality, the process of childbirth and the process of writing a novel. Even Tom Campbell—who was mightily pleased to have a real author in his small bailiwick—seemed to recognize that Scott's speech was as dull a piece of work as anyone was likely to hear in Hamilton. (With the exception, unacknowledged by Tom, of his own perorations.)

At the circulation desk, where Susan Miles had joined her, Dewey began to rack her brains for a polite and appropriate way to bring Alfred to a halt.

"Ring the fire alarm, Dewey," suggested Susan, sotto voce.

"Do something," pleaded George.

But Dewey was spared intervention as Henrietta Ambler's voice rang out in tones of thundering authority. "Charming, Alfred dear. But that will do." She led the crowd in a round of applause.

George handed Dewey his glass. "Uh-oh. Here comes trouble. Make it a double, my dear." Henrietta Ambler, having silenced her son-in-law, was heading their way.

"Afternoon, Henrietta," said George with a straight face.

"George. Dewey. What a bore that man is. How Abby could have stood him for so long, I'll never know." She held out her glass. "Make mine vermouth, Dewey, there's a dear." Dewey filled Henrietta Ambler's glass, and the wealthy widow sipped at her drink idly, looking around. Finally she turned on George. "Don't you snicker at me, George Farnham."

"Snicker?" George's face was full of innocence. "Henrietta, what on earth do you mean?"

"I'm sure Dewey has told you every detail." She glanced at Susan Miles. "Susan, run along, there's a dear." Susan Miles choked back a laugh and departed. Henrietta glowered at Farnham. "Don't you ever play the fool with me, George."

"I wouldn't dream of it, Henrietta," he replied, with a wink at Dewey.

"Fortunately, I spoke to Gerald Davidson this morning. It appears that he has been worrying about this matter ever since he left town on Sunday. I told him what Fielding Booker had been up to, and he set my mind at rest. He had already started his own investigation. At what he so charmingly calls 'the highest level.' He's a fool, that man.

But I have discovered that when I need a favor, there is no one more willing to oblige than a senator with a half-empty campaign chest." She laughed.

Dewey was shocked. "You don't mean to say you've gone over Bookie's head, Henrietta?"

"Don't I, though?" She looked placidly back at Dewey. "Dewey, really. You don't for one minute suppose Fielding Booker is capable of solving these crimes?" Dewey glanced toward Booker, who had been cornered by Mary Barstow. He appeared to be attending to the dental hygienist with his customary politeness; but Dewey, who knew Booker very well indeed, recognized the look on his face. It was an SOS.

"Come, now, Henrietta, I think you have gone too far. I really do. Bookie is a very able man."

"Hah. Dewey, darling, he's positively floundering. Absolutely in over his head. But don't you worry. Gerald told me that somebody had an idea about this whole silly affair. He'll get to the bottom of it. Without any more bumbling."

"Good gracious!" Dewey suddenly had had enough of Henrietta Ambler. "Really, Henrietta. I think that is most unfair."

"Do you, Dewey? Isn't that rather the pot and the kettle?" She put down her glass. "I think I've done my bit for my son-in-law. Lovely party, Dewey." She pulled on a bright green silk jacket and departed.

"Heaven to Betsy!" said Dewey. "I wonder if Bookie knows."

"Bound to," replied George. "What do you say we cheer him up, Dewey. With a cozy little dinner for three, *chez moi*?"

"Oh, dear. No—George. You go right ahead. I have a million and one things to do."

"Is that right?"

"Yes," replied Dewey firmly.

"All right, my dear." He glanced over toward Abby Scott. "I must say, the author's wife doesn't look any too happy this afternoon."

Dewey followed his glance. Abby Scott was leaning up against the biography bookcase. In one hand was a glass of sherry, in the other advance copy of *Blues*. She was regarding her husband with an unhappy, glassy-eyed stare. "I see what you mean," replied Dewey. "I wonder what on earth can be the matter. She brought me some azalea bushes this morning and looked as happy as a clam. Seemed rather proud of Alfred and his book, you know."

As they watched, Abby Scott detached herself slowly from the bookcase. She put her drink down on a nearby table, placed the book next to it, and headed for the front door.

"George! She's leaving! You stay right here with the refreshments." Dewey scurried out from behind the desk and followed Abby Scott out into the cool late-afternoon air.

She caught up with her on the pavement outside. "Abby!"

Abby Scott turned. "Hi, Mrs. James."

"Abby, dear, whatever is the matter?"

"Nothing. Just wanted a little air, that's all."

Dewey took her arm. "Come, come, dear. You know better than that."

Abby Scott sighed. "Mrs. James, I think there's something wrong with Alfred."

"Whatever do you mean, child?"

"He's—I think he's been lying to me. Mrs. James, I think he's having an affair."

"Oh, good heavens. That's impossible. Alfred?"

Abby smiled. "I know he's not exactly a prize. But you know, Mrs. James, some women will do anything to get their claws into another woman's husband."

Into Dewey's mind flashed a picture of Mary Barstow, smiling cozily up at Alfred. But even Alfred Scott was man enough, surely, to withstand Mary Barstow's clumsy and cloying advances.

"Come on, Abby. Whatever you may think, this isn't the time for it. You and Alfred must sort this out in private."

"I suppose you're right, Mrs. James."

They returned to the sherry party, where Alfred Scott was distinctly enjoying his celebrity. George and Bookie departed, and Dewey looked around with pleasure. It really was going very nicely. There was no threat of further speeches by Tom Campbell or Alfred Scott. She settled in behind the circulation desk and talked cozily to Susan Miles about local affairs.

"Terrific party, Dewey."

"It is rather a lot of fun, having an author in our midst."

"And quite an improvement over last week's little gathering. Tom's friend is gone, I take it."

"Yes, he is—and not a moment too soon. Susan, do you know I think that man must be very unhappy. As Blake said, 'A horse misused upon the road/Calls to heaven for human blood.' "

"Oooh. Don't remind me. There was something really awful about that night—the way he rubbed his hands together."

"George hated the way he licked his lips."

"Ugh. That too! Don't remind me. I'll have nightmares again, Dewey."

Dewey smiled. "You really ought to trade in General Barker for a better model of dog, Susan. You can rent Isaiah for the night, if you're still worried about Renfrew's ghosts."

Susan laughed. "I'll just force Nick to look after me properly, that's all."

The party went on late into the evening. Abby Scott departed early, but Alfred stayed on, relishing his celebrity and achievement. At nine o'clock Dewey yawned. It really was time to go home. She left Tom Campbell and Alfred Scott to their cheerful inebriety and headed for her car.

As she drove out the long winding course of Hillside Road to her house, Dewey felt a slight chill of fear. She wished that Susan hadn't reminded her about Professor Renfrew and his pictures of blood sacrifice. It really was strange, the way that Jenny Riley's death had followed his gruesome lecture. There had been something tense and unreal about the whole of last Friday evening.

She tried not to think about it, but the image of the little professor, with his milky spectacles and air of macabre satisfaction, seemed to dance before her in the dark as she drove. It seemed that there was something about that night that had eluded her. There was *something* buried in her mind—a significant fact that would make sense of all the rest.

And by the time she reached home, Dewey had realized what it was. She knew, now, who had to have murdered Jenny Riley and Norman Fox—and why.

"Isaiah, old boy," she remarked to her dog as she filled his dinner bowl. "I have had an *éclaircissement*, which is not a dessert but an inspiration. Memory, you know, is the warder of the mind."

Now all she had to do was work out a way to trap the killer. Perhaps, if she was very persuasive, she could enlist Bookie's aid. He would want to be in at the moment of truth.

27

"BOOKIE? ARE YOU listening?"

"Yes, Dewey."

"Well? What do you think?"

"It's an interesting idea, Dewey. And I don't mind telling you that I have just about run out of ideas in this little affair. You say you want me to get Mildred Jones in here for questioning?"

"Yes. I'll be along in a little while—I need to take care of one or two details. I don't suppose Officer Machen spoke to Amy Freeman, by the way?"

"Amy who?"

"I thought so. I'll be there in half an hour, Bookie."

She rang off and climbed in the car. The first stop would be Jensen's Feed & Grain.

The bell above the door tinkled as Dewey entered the old shop.

"Morning, Mrs. James," said Rob Jensen, looking up from his account books. "Do something for you today?" He was a good-looking, burly man, rather taciturn and set in his ways, but widely liked by his customers.

"Hello, Rob. Yes—you can. Or, that is to say, I hope you can."

"Starbuck doing well, is she?"

"Oh, yes, indeed. Never been brighter." Rob Jensen had been supplying oats and hay to horse breeders in the area for twenty years; Dewey had a running account with him for a special kind of feed for Starbuck—something called The

Old Gray Mare. Dewey felt that Starbuck enjoyed it very much. "No, it was about that aphid spray." Dewey stepped up to the counter. "I believe that you carry a kind called Aphids Away?"

Jensen nodded. "Yes, ma'am, but like I told Officer Machen, when he come in here about it, I haven't sold a can of that stuff in two or three years. It's over there, right up there with the weed killer, which I also don't sell. I oughtta give the whole dang shelfful to Abby Scott. Nobody comes here for that kind of thing anymore."

Dewey stepped over to the shelf and took a look. There was indeed the dust of ages on the tops of all the cans of the nicotine preparation. But in one corner there was a gap, and the dust on the shelf had been disturbed.

"Rob. Please come and have a look."

Jensen obliged. When he saw what Dewey was looking at, he let out a whistle. "Well, I'll be danged if I wasn't robbed." He shook his head. "I suppose I better let Captain Booker know right away."

"Rob—what about Amy?"

There was a sudden light in Jensen's eyes. "Mrs. James, I think you might just be right. Let's look." He hastened to the counter and pulled out a huge old ledger book. "You know, I just didn't think of her. Nobody ever comes in here on a Thursday afternoon."

"I think you may have had a customer last Thursday, Rob."

They quickly turned up Amy Freeman's single entry in the book. Beside it, in a round and cheerful hand, was a note to Jensen: "Look, Boss—a Sale. How about a raise?" Jensen smiled as he read the note. "Nine eighty-seven," he said, turning to his calculator. "With tax, that's just exactly right, Mrs. James."

"Rob. This is very important. This murderer has struck twice, you know. You'll have to close the shop right away and go get Amy. She may be in danger. Will you bring her to the police station?"

"Right away, Mrs. James." He locked the register and turned the Open sign in the doorway around, then roared off down the road toward Hamilton High. Dewey, equally anxious but always a careful driver, moved at a slower pace toward town.

There was pandemonium in the police station when Dewey arrived. As she opened the door, she could hear Mildred Jones's voice above the rest of the clamor. "What right have you got to drag me down here like I was some kind of criminal? You're the one ought to be locked up. I never laid a hand on that girl."

"Hush, Mrs. Jones, please," came Booker's voice. He sounded exasperated. Dewey hoped to heaven her plan wouldn't be scotched by this woman. She followed the noise down the hall to Booker's office and poked her head in at the door.

"Good morning, Mildred," she said, interrupting Mildred Jones's tirade. The woman whirled on her.

"You! You filthy, snooping, prying old—"

"That will *do*!" thundered Booker. He sat and put his head in his hands. Why on earth had he ever agreed to this cockamamy scheme of this lunatic, Dewey James? "Dewey, do something about this. Please."

"Certainly, Bookie. Mildred. Sit down. Nobody in here has accused you of anything—have they?"

"I'd like to know what you call being hauled off my job in a police car, then, Mrs. Dewey Snoopface James." She turned on Booker and extended her wrists. "Go on, put the handcuffs on. Then get Sonny Royce down here to take a picture of the poor widow woman being arrested for murder. Everybody in this town knows you're only trying to save your own hide from the electric chair."

"Mildred, stop it at once." Dewey's voice was icy. It was the tone she resorted to in the library when things got too far out of hand in the teen readers room; she had never in her life used it on an adult. But it had never failed; it didn't fail her now. Mildred Jones clamped her mouth shut tight and sat down, glaring.

"That's better," said Dewey. Sergeant Fenton, curious about the sudden quiet, peeked in. He grinned at Dewey.

"Mildred. We need your help. Yours and Tommy's."

"Hah. Tommy's? Everybody in town knows Tommy's disgrace."

"What on earth are you talking about? Mildred—Tommy hasn't been disgraced. He has been unwell. We all are unwell from time to time. But you really must understand this, if he is to get better."

Booker looked sourly out the window. The last thing he wanted was some soap opera on mental health in his office. He cleared his throat peremptorily. "Ladies. Shall we get to the business of the morning?"

"Right away, Bookie," said Dewey, giving him a look. "Mildred," she said gently, "I would like to arrange for Tommy to visit. But before he comes, you must tell him about Jenny's death. And I think perhaps you ought to speak to his doctors, to make certain that someone looks after him. It will be a terrible blow."

"If you know so much about Tommy, lady, why don't you tell him?"

"Because I'm only the town librarian, Mildred. You're his mother. Please."

Mildred Jones looked warily from one to the other. "What if I don't want to?"

"Well, Mildred, if you don't, you don't. But I doubt that Tommy will ever forgive you if you shirk this duty."

There was a long silence in the little room. At last Mildred Jones nodded. "Okay."

"Do it this morning, Mildred. Right now." Dewey looked at Booker, who caught the question in her eye. He rose and gestured to his desk.

"Please, Mildred. You can use my phone. We'll step out into the hallway."

He and Dewey left the little office and closed the door behind them. They waited tensely for twenty minutes, and Dewey related to Booker her discovery at Jensen's Feed & Grain.

"Went on a Thursday. Wouldn't you know it. Huh." He shook his head and looked around. "Machen!"

Fenton looked up from the front desk. "It's his day off, sir."

"I'll day-off him, I will, Mike. You get him on the horn right now. I want to see him ASAP."

"Yessir."

Mildred Jones came out of the office at last. Her face was tear-stained, but she looked somehow restored. Dewey wondered how long it had been since she'd heard Tommy's voice.

"Mildred, why don't I give you a lift home?" asked Dewey.

"There's no need, really, Mrs. James. I have to go back to work, anyway." She swallowed hard. "Tommy's doctor says it would be good for him to come home. Says he can get him here by tomorrow. Thinks it might make it more real, or something, about Jenny."

"The funeral is tomorrow. Will he be here in time?"

"Yes. Oh, Mrs. James." Mildred Jones flung herself at Dewey and began to sob in earnest. Dewey stroked the woman's hair softly, then walked with her outside.

"I'm sorry about what I said in there," Mildred Jones said at last. "I was just so frightened."

"It's all right, Mildred. I think I know why."

"You do?"

Dewey nodded. "You were hoping to put an end to Jenny's success, weren't you?"

"I—I—"

"Come on, Mildred. I promise you that your secret will be safe with me. You are the person who called Isadora Hebb and sent Jenny an invitation to the Homecoming. Because you had thought of a way to make her suffer."

"I don't know what you mean."

"And when she got here," Dewey went on, "you knew exactly which room was hers. On Saturday, after the River Festival, you returned to the inn and coated the tub in Jenny's room with butcher's wax. You wanted Jenny to break a leg, didn't you?"

The bitterness had drained out of Mildred Jones's face,

but her old stubbornness had returned. "There's no proof of anything."

"No, there isn't. And believe me, Mildred, I won't say a word to anyone. Now. Would you like someone to meet Tommy tomorrow at the airport?"

"I'll go."

"George will be glad to go with you."

"I said I will go. He's my boy. Good-bye, Mrs. James."

Dewey watched as Mildred Jones marched up the street toward the Hamilton Inn. "Go, bind your son to exile," murmured Dewey with bitterness. She entered the police station once more.

28

ROB JENSEN HAD arrived with a shaken Amy Freeman under his arm. They were now seated in Booker's office with Dewey; Sergeant Fenton had brought in extra chairs, and the little room was very crowded. The mood was intense.

"Very good, Miss Freeman," Booker was saying. "We understand very well. You were speaking on the telephone with your friend, er—"

"Helene McGrath," put in Fenton, reading back from his notes.

"Yes. A Miss McGrath. A man entered the store and complained to you briefly of aphids. But you didn't engage him in any sort of conversation. You know—'Good afternoon,' 'Can I help you?' or even 'Nice day'—is that correct?"

"Well, not really." She looked at Jensen for help.

"It's okay, Amy. I told you you could use the phone."

Amy Freeman gulped and went on. "No. I mean, we were talking about the Homecoming Dance. Phil and I are like really into dancing, and we thought we might win." She glanced at Dewey. "I mean, I did talk to the guy. Told him where to look, in that big blue book that Rob always looks things up in."

"But you didn't recognize him?"

"Well—I mean, he was wearing a hat—a Hornets cap—and sunglasses. And I didn't really look at his face."

"Describe him, please, the best you can."

"He was—kind of medium. You know?"

Booker sighed. "Do you think, Miss Freeman, that you would recognize this person again?"

"Yeah. Maybe." She looked hopeful.

Booker shook his head. *Maybe* wasn't good enough. If they held a line-up, and this girl failed to pick him out, they'd be up a stump.

"Bookie," said Dewey. "I wonder if I might have a word with you?"

He gave her a skeptical glance, then rose. They stepped out into the hall; Dewey pulled the door to Booker's office shut behind her. "Bookie—you know, I think if we set this up properly, it may not matter if Amy Freeman recognizes him."

"What do you mean? Come on, Dewey—that girl is our star witness. Without her the whole thing falls apart."

"Not necessarily. Not if he *thinks* he's been recognized. You might be able to get a confession out of him. May I suggest a little pantomime, for the funeral tomorrow?" She outlined her idea.

"It's risky, Dewey," said Booker.

"Well, of course it is. But if it doesn't work, you can still go through months of police procedure. This might be a good shortcut. And it will get Gerald Davidson off your back."

Booker sighed. "It will put our suspect on his guard."

"So be it," said Dewey. "He won't erase whatever evidence there may be. What's done cannot be undone."

They returned to the office. "Fenton, put your notes away, son."

"Sir."

"Mrs. James has made a suggestion. I would like it to be perfectly clear to all of you present that what she proposes is ex-officio. In fact—Fenton, you and I had better clear out."

"Sir."

They went, leaving Dewey to explain her ideas to the two who were left.

29

THE OBSEQUIES FOR Jenny Riley were exceedingly well attended. Her celebrity in life might have on its own guaranteed a crowd; but she had been apotheosized by her tragic death in her little hometown. In addition to the many friends who truly grieved for her, there were dozens of townsfolk who had come from simple respect, simple curiosity, or perhaps simplemindedness. There were those, too, who came to drink in the atmosphere of sadness and mystery that surrounded the funeral of one who had died so young and unexpectedly. Dewey was not at all surprised to see that Professor Renfrew had turned up; he seemed gratified, in his ghastly way, and took notes throughout the service.

Jack Riley had gone to the Seven Locks Tavern for the better part of the morning. Thus fortified, he bore his position in the spotlight well. He had asked George Farnham to be the chief pallbearer; and George, with the generosity of a true friend, had taken it upon himself to organize the entire ceremony.

Alfred and Abby Scott were seated in the pew across the aisle from Dewey. She glanced over at them and was surprised to see that Henrietta Ambler had decided to attend. Dewey suppressed a smile as she followed Henrietta's gaze to the front pew, where the pallbearers were seated. Even from this distance, Dewey could easily distinguish Alejandro Ponseca, by the set of his head, the grace of the back of his neck. He was really quite a man.

Dewey wondered if, in Henrietta Ambler, Ponseca had

somehow finally met his match. As long as Booker kept his promise—extracted earlier this morning—never to reveal Ponseca's secret, Henrietta Ambler would love him. Dewey stifled a laugh as she recollected the contents of the long-awaited report from Baltimore. Ponseca, it turned out, was no Latin lover, after all. He was Vince Fenn, the son and heir of Rory Fenn, Baltimore's King of Kustom Plastik Slipkovers. Ah, well. His secret was safe enough.

Mildred Jones was there, of course. She looked shaken and, thought Dewey, perhaps really sorry for Jenny's death. Dewey wondered if Mildred felt responsible. She had, after all, been the one to send the Homecoming invitation. But Dewey felt that this murderer would have acted, sooner or later, in Hamilton or in New York. It wasn't Mildred's fault.

Seated next to his mother, upright and very still in a dark suit, Tommy Jones looked old beyond his years. He was pale and thin, without a sign of his old spark. But Dewey thought about the letter he had written his mother and the scathing reference to a two-handed bridge game. She felt sure that Tommy would be all right; she hoped it wouldn't take very long.

Alejandro Ponseca made a short and eloquent speech about Jenny. He framed it all in dancing images, so that the beautiful young girl seemed to turn and whirl before them once more; not stilled by death, but still turning, turning, with flashing eyes and a bright and generous smile.

They read the Twenty-third Psalm; Susan Miles, seated next to Dewey, squeezed her hand for comfort. And then it was over. The congregation poured out of the little frame church and onto the street out front.

Dewey looked. Fielding Booker had been as good as his word. He was there, leaning up against the side of the car; next to him was Amy Freeman. They watched carefully as the little group around Dewey filtered out through the door into the beautiful sunshine. Professor Renfrew stepped out and blinked, twice, in the sunlight. Dewey kept her eyes fixed on Amy. It was critical to give no hint.

Suddenly Amy grabbed Booker's arm and began to nod

earnestly. She pointed, nodded again. Booker moved toward the crowd.

Alfred Scott, caught up in the press of people, began to panic. He hurried through, squeezing past the mourners, pushing rudely past Jack Riley. "Alfred? Alfred!" called Henrietta Ambler in her deepest tone of authority. "Abby, what on earth is wrong with that man?"

Alfred Scott broke free of the crowd and began to sprint in earnest. He looked behind him. Fielding Booker was following at a sure-paced, leisurely trot. Alfred Scott tried to breathe, but it seemed that breath wouldn't come. His lungs were burning. And what had happened to his legs? They had turned to air; disappeared. He pumped away, a driven animal, a hunted animal, but there was no substance beneath him, only air. His muscles and sinews were gone, replaced by an insubstantial nightmare, a joke. Run—he must run, run, run—

Sergeant Mike Fenton was waiting at the corner. He stepped out into Scott's path, spreading his arms wide. "Gotcha," said Sergeant Mike Fenton.

30

"Now, JUST ONE minute, Dewey James," said Henrietta Ambler. "I won't have you leaving things out of this story of yours. We've heard all about the poison and so forth from George, but now it's your turn. Good God Almighty, I knew that man was lame. But *murder*. Honestly. You would think he hadn't been properly raised. I must know, Dewey. How on earth did you guess?"

"That was no guess," objected George Farnham, who was handing round the hors d'oeuvres. For once a crowd had gathered in George's living room, instead of his kitchen. "Dewey reasoned it all through. Didn't you, my dear?"

"Well, I—"

"I bet you did," said Tommy Jones with a smile. He was perched on a large leather footstool, and he looked worn but much better than he had earlier in the day. "Nobody ever put one over on Dewey James. I should know."

"Indeed you should, young man," agreed Dewey. "No one ever tried harder than you."

"Stop this nonsense at once. Alejandro—make them stop. I want to hear Dewey's story." Henrietta Ambler, seated next to Ponseca on the sofa, smiled at the dancer.

Ponseca winked at Dewey. "If you would be so very kind, Señora James, to reward our curiosity with the facts?"

"Well." Dewey took a deep breath. "You see, the other night it came to me in a flash—what I like to call an *éclaircissement*. Except, this time, it was literally that. A light. We had all forgotten that the whole time Jenny was

179

dancing for us, Alfred was up on the gallery, operating the spotlight. I only remembered the other night, after Alfred's sherry party. I was thinking about how he had helped, the week before, with the slide projector and so forth. And then I remembered that he had been running the spotlight in the Great Hall."

"That Fielding Booker ought to be fired. Don't you think, George?" Henrietta Ambler gazed at George fiercely.

George Farnham shook his head. "My word, Henrietta. You're as much to blame as poor old Bookie. If you had only left the man in peace to do his job, instead of calling in that idiot Davidson—"

"Dewey still would have been the one to work it out," finished Henrietta Ambler. "Go on, Dewey. George was being rude. He interrupted you."

Dewey chuckled and continued her tale. "When I thought of that, everything fell into place. You know as well as I do that Alfred could no more write a book than fly to the moon."

"I do," agreed Henrietta Ambler.

"Everyone knew that. We all kept remarking on how astonishing it was that he was being published. George more or less accused him of stealing the book, right in the library on the night that Professor Renfrew gave his ghastly talk. You remember, George. You said that he had lifted the whole story, or something like that."

"So I did," replied George, gratified to be included in the denouement. "Very helpful little insight, wasn't it?"

"Yes. And then, you know—there we all were, standing around, talking about his book. He was pleased as Punch. Until Jenny and Mr. Ponseca joined our little group. Then he changed the subject. 'Enough about me,' he said, or some such nonsense. Jenny made him terribly uncomfortable." She looked at Tommy Jones. "Because, of all the people in the world, Jenny was the only one who knew, for certain, that the book was not Alfred's at all, but Tommy's."

"Charming," said Henrietta Ambler. She shook her head. "How Abby could—"

"Oh, now, Henrietta. Don't blame Abby. We all are

subject to the blandishments of emotions that we neither comprehend nor control. He was her husband. She loved him." Dewey privately thought that anyone at all would have seemed, to Abby, like a lifeboat. Anything to escape the tyranny of the S.S. *Henrietta Ambler*.

"Well, Dewey, suppose you explain to us exactly how he got hold of the book. In language you comprehend and control." Henrietta Ambler smiled.

"Oh, that was easy. You see, Jenny remembered, when Tommy had finished his manuscript, that Alfred had been an agent at one time. Not a very good agent, perhaps—but still, he knew a few people in the publishing world. I think that she simply telephoned him one day to ask for a bit of friendly advice, and he offered to read it."

"He did more than just read it," put in George Farnham.

Dewey nodded. "That's right. I'm afraid, Henrietta, that Alfred really ought to be ashamed of himself. Deeply. He recognized that Tommy's manuscript had a great deal of promise. And, thinking perhaps that Tommy would never know the difference, he submitted it to a publisher—all the while pretending he had written it himself."

"The loathsome little tick!" exclaimed Henrietta Ambler. She downed the last of her martini and glowered at Dewey, who continued.

"Yes," agreed Dewey, rather ruefully. "It was a nasty trick to play. When Harbison House said they'd publish *Blues*, it was too good a chance for Alfred to pass up. I imagine he rationalized it; told himself that he would make everything all right, or that Harbison House wouldn't have taken it if they'd known it was Tommy's." She glanced apologetically in Tommy's direction; but that young man, for all his recent misfortune, seemed to bear up well under this tale of treachery. Perhaps, for Tommy Jones, one more betrayal in life was small potatoes.

"That's exactly right," added George Farnham. "Bookie told me as much this afternoon. It was all in Alfred's statement."

"You mean Alfred has *confessed*?" Henrietta Ambler was stunned. "He just rolled over like a dog and confessed?

And Tommy here was the real author? Ooh! I told you, Dewey, Alfred's a newt. Worse than a newt. A whatsit—crustacean. No backbone."

"I would have to agree with you on that point, Henrietta," put in George. "First time you and I have seen eye to eye in many a year. How about another drink, on the strength of that?"

"Make mine very dry, George. With an olive."

"George," said Dewey with a mischievous smile, "I believe you might make an excellent replacement for Brant. Didn't you say your butler was leaving, Henrietta?"

"Oh, shut up, Dewey, and talk," replied Henrietta Ambler.

While George refilled the glasses, Dewey continued with her story.

"Well, I began to think about people who might have some connection to Jenny in New York. There, I admit, I was very stupid indeed. I couldn't get it out of my mind that Norman Fox knew something. Which he did, of course—he knew that Alfred had been up on the gallery. In fact, he had gone up to the gallery to talk to Alfred. And he worked it out that Alfred was the most likely person to have access to Jenny's room while the dancing was going on."

"What on earth would Alfred have to say to that little man?" Henrietta Ambler was dismayed.

"Oh, something about horses, I expect. Or perhaps the numbers. Bookie told George that the New York police turned up Norman Fox's file—he was calling himself Herman Wolf there."

"How original."

"Yes. He was nearly caught a year ago, running some kind of gambling thing. And I believe he had seen Jenny and Alfred together in New York, at one point. Jenny, of course, was famous. Perhaps Alfred had even placed a bet or two with Fox, on one of his trips to see his publisher. Tommy's publisher, I should say."

"Yes. Tommy's publisher," agreed Ponseca handsomely. He raised his glass. "To *Blues*."

Tommy grinned, then looked at Dewey. "Hey, Mrs. James. How come Jenny never tumbled to it?"

"To what, young man?" interjected Henrietta Ambler.

"That he had stolen my book."

"Simple," said George. "He kept telling her he was shopping it around. He couldn't give it back, you know, on the off-chance that you might sell it yourself."

"And I rather suspect, Tommy," put in Dewey, "that Alfred had pretty primitive notions about your mental state. It would be just your word against his, if you ever challenged him. I imagine he relied on the prejudices of the world, to believe his story, if it ever came to that. In the meantime, he saw easy money. It's a very good book."

"How much money?" asked Henrietta Ambler.

"Oh, really, Henrietta."

"Answer me, Dewey. I have a very good reason for wanting to know."

George stepped in. "Well, the advance, according to Booker, was substantial. Hundred thousand, or so. But the royalties will probably bring in three or four times that much."

"My goodness, Tommy," said Dewey. She was impressed. "Are they really going to publish it, George?"

"Looks that way. Booker put in a call to the editor today, as soon as he could. It's all printed and ready to go—on its way to a bookstore near you. Probably be good for sales, all this business. Sad but true."

"Well," said Henrietta Ambler, rising. "We must be off, George. Coming, darling?" She looked at Ponseca, who rose. "Thank you, Dewey, for your interesting story. Good-bye, young man," she said to Tommy. "I am heartily glad that book is yours and not Alfred's. I would so hate to have to respect him for anything." She glanced at Ponseca, who was holding Dewey's hand and looking deeply into her eyes.

"Do you remember, Señora James, what we talked of, when we spoke of love that day?"

"I do, indeed, Mr. Ponseca. Of course." Dewey turned pink and carefully avoided George's eye.

"I think you are a truly remarkable beauty." He leaned in closer to whisper. "And, if I had but time—"

"Enough, Alejandro." Henrietta Ambler led him away. George escorted his guests to the door.

"I better go, too, Mrs. James," said Tommy. "I wanted to say thank you. From me, and my mother. She didn't quite know how to do it herself."

"Thank *you*, Tommy." Dewey looked fondly at him. "Are you all right?"

"Getting there. Jenny was a big help. She was the best friend a person could want."

"I think she felt that way about you, too, Tommy."

"Do you?"

"Yes. Mr. Ponseca said that she felt your life was in her hands; and that it made her afraid and happy at the same time."

"I know just what that feels like."

"Well, well, my dear," said George, when Tommy was gone. "You made short work of all that. What do you say to a little dinner? And, after dinner, I shall take you dancing." George smiled his sweetest smile, held out his arm to Dewey, and led her happily into the kitchen.

A few months later George Farnham was opening his mail at the town council office. He was surprised to find in the morning's post a letter from Henrietta Ambler—that is, Henrietta Ponseca. It had been sent from Curaçao, where she and Alejandro Ponseca were honeymooning. He thought of them briefly with envy, and laughed out loud when he recalled what Dewey had told him about Ponseca's origins. Vince Fenn, the Crown Prince of the King of Kustom Plastik Slipkovers. George wiped a tear of mirth from his eye and opened the letter with curiosity.

George:
   I wanted to do something about that poor girl. Enclosed is a little bit of seed capital. When we get back to Hamilton, Alejandro is going to go to work

(he's terribly lazy at heart, you know). We are setting up the Jenny Riley Dance Foundation. He'll give you the details. Put this in the bank for now.

Love to Dewey. Why don't you persuade her to take a honeymoon with you, George? Of course you'd have to get her to marry you first. But for what it's worth, I recommend it highly.

Henrietta Ponseca

George looked at the check and whistled. Then he looked back at Henrietta's letter and laughed out loud.

"Ahh, Henrietta," said George with a chuckle. "If only you knew."